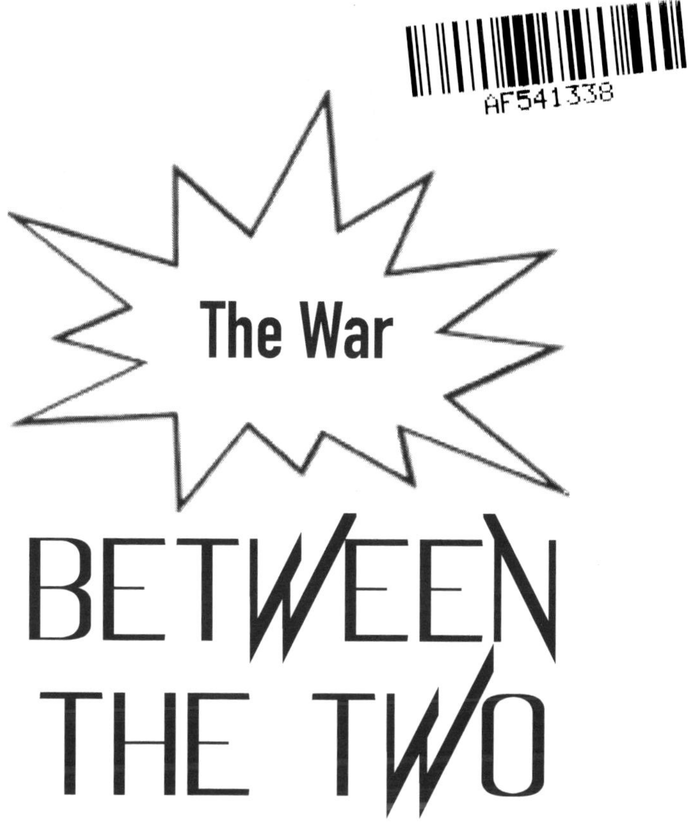

Adeep S.L

Invincible Publishers

First published in India in 2017 by Invincible Publishers

ISBN: 978-93-86148-30-8

Invincible Publishers
F-55, Sushant Lok II, Hong Kong Bazar Lane Sector 57, Gurgaon-122003

Opposite Kasturba Ashram, Radaur Distt Yamuna Nagar, Haryana- 135133

About the Author

❄ ❄ ❄

Adeep Srinivasa Seshan Lakshmi or usually known by his pen name Adeep S.L is an Indian writer born on 4th of August in the year 2002. Adeep, who is now doing his schooling in Dubai, had the passion of writing from the age of 10. At the age of thirteen, he had written his first book which was titled *I do not understand a thing* and was published last year.

Adeep likes exploring new things. He does not want his ideas to be restricted to only four walls and wants to share it with the world.

The war between the two is his second book and he hopes to create more worlds of books with his pen and paper.

Index

Preface

❄ ❄ ❄

The war between the two is a book that will be etched in my memory for years to come. This particular story has been lying around in my creative desktop from the age of eleven and was a great deal to get it into the world of literature.

Three years ago, it was a simple thought that sparked in my mind. I then started to build on that element captured by me in my dreaming session. I used to visualise each and every scene in my story and it led me to more and more questions, which I began to answer. Now at last, I have my story fit and ready. The book takes you through swashbuckling move made by two great competitors in their own game. That's what made it the war between the two.

Adro Whyson was a character I enjoyed creating. This story portrays Adro's wits and Hobad's shrewdness, which makes their battle out of the ordinary. If I were to tell which was the toughest part of the book was, then I would say that getting a title for each chapter was the challenging part. Nevertheless, I thoroughly enjoyed the process.

Last but not the least; I would like to thank everyone responsible for making this book possible. Without them, I couldn't have discovered the unknown side of myself.

INTRODUCTION

❄ ❄ ❄

Based extensively in the fictional country of Masnesia, This is a story that revolves around two rich, powerful and influential people, Adro Whyson and Hobad Doughnauts. Hobad has always been cold towards Adro right from their childhood due to his inferiority complex.

Years after, the feud is still on with both Adro and Hobad. Both are placed at great positions in society. But eventually Adro meets with an accident and soon discovers something new, something different and something so unique that has never been talked about anywhere.

But with these new and unique powers of his, what will Adro do? Is he going to be a saint or a sinner?

Here we go

October 2016 - Chennai

* * *

It's a partially cloudy morning, Eprun Tapeboy rushes to the Chennai central to catch the train to Bangalore that would depart at 15 minutes to four in the afternoon. He starts running towards the second platform at which the Shatabdi express was standing to travel the 350 kilometre ride to Bangalore.

He quickly scanned the paper stuck outside each compartment of the train for the passengers to view the seating reservation. "Oh that's great!" Exclaimed Eprun, "I have the window seat". He was also relaxed to spot out that departure of the train is delayed by another 10 minutes. Eprun decided to walk towards the nearest tea stall to have a cup of tea. He ordered a cup of tea and a butter biscuit and handed over the ten rupee note to the cashier.

Eprun sat down on the bench of the semi-open tea stall and got himself a newspaper to read. Just as he was about to open the newspaper, he spotted a man who was like Eprun, with a single suitcase and ordered himself a tea too. As soon as Eprun saw him, he realised that he was from Eprun's college. "Hello Junward Bouchard. How are you?" The man turned around and was delighted to spot Eprun, "Hi Eprun, What makes you here."

"I had a meeting over here. So I just came for a day."

"Oh that's great. So where are you heading to?"

"Back to Bangalore"

"Is it? I am going out there to meet my friend." Junward replied. "So tell me, How are things then for you?" Junward asked and Eprun replied with a smile, "With me everything is good, I am just enjoying myself and visiting from state to state and country to country. I am just..." Eprun noticed a change in expression in Junward.

From a happy and excited face, his face was now filled with apprehension. "What happened?" asked Eprun. Junward was shivering from inside and slowly began to raise his hands up and uttered in fright. "Eprun... Just turn back for a moment" Eprun slowly turned back and was horrified.

Behind him were a group of goons, with their revolvers aiming at Eprun. "So you are Eprun Tapeboy, right?" A goon asked, with a hard and high pitched voice. "Yes. I am Eprun." The goon replied with an Indian accent. He was not well versed with Englsih and spoke out whatever he knew. "Okay, do remember you the Hobad." "The who?" Eprun asked. "Arey can't you hear me. The Hobad. The Hobad Doughnauts" Shouted the goon in irritation and confusion of speaking an unknown language. "Yes, I do know him. He was my schoolmate. What's the matter?" Eprun inquired.

"Guys, so he is the Eprun. Take charge!" The goon shouted and all of a sudden all the goons unlock their revolvers and made themselves ready to pull the trigger. "Three" The head started the countdown. "Two, One and......"

Before he could say go, the Commander was kicked on his leg causing him to fall down and his revolver was immediately grabbed by Eprun. He pointed the revolver towards the leader's head and shouted, "Put your guns down!" "No one should move from their present position."

The Commander started to shout in fright, "Just listen to him, and put it down." The whole clan immediately dropped down their guns. "That's good." Eprun replied with a smile on his face. He swapped the revolver from his left hand to his right and had a look at his watch.

"Now it should start." He announced and set himself to pull the triggers. As he was about to do it, Junward shouted, "Eprun, the train has started to move." Eprun did not react. He was still and steady.

As he heard the train move quicker, as fast as a tracer bullet, he threw the machine on the face of the head and shouted, "Junward, RUN!!" Eprun then turned back, picked up his suitcase and ran towards the train with Junward.

The Commander commanded them to follow the two and catch them alive. Eprun gave his full potential to chase the train and was about to catch the train. As soon as the two of them got inside the compartment, the train started to catch up and fle away from them. "Oh no!" cried the Commander. "We missed him."

Inside the compartment, Junward was busy

searching for his seat and was also palpitating from inside. "What's the matter? You are searching for your seat?" Asked Eprun, Who was exhausted too and removed a bottle of water and sat down on his allotted seat. "Yes Eprun, My seat number is 55." "55!!" Eprun exclaimed. Then here is your seat." Eprun stated pointing to the seat next to him.

"Oh! Next to you." A frightened Junward exclaimed and sat down at his allocated seat. "Want water?" Asked Eprun. "Yes, Thanks a lot" Junward grabbed the bottle and had a sip of it. "Eprun, who were they?" asked Junward. "They were the goons of Hobad Doughnauts." Replied Eprun.

"Hobad? Who is the owner and CEO of Banana Electronics?"

"Yes. It's him."

"Why does he need to kill you?"

"It's because of Whyson, Adro Whyson."

"Wait, Wait, Wait" Junward said. "It's 2 years since Adro is missing and he has also been accused as a psychopathic robber and a murderer. Why would he need to kill you then?"

"That's because I was with Adro." stated Eprun. "I do not understand a thing. You are just complicating stuffs." replied Junward.

"Okay then. I will explain everything. It's a long story though." warned Eprun. "It's a five hour journey mate. You can go on."

"Thank you very much Junward. Let's start then."

The War ! !

* * *

Masnesia is an island country located below the Arabian Peninsula. The land span was over five hundred and forty two kilometres. This country has two provinces; one is the Masnesia city, a desert that has become a concrete jungle with super high structures and also a trading hub for the country of Masnesia.

The second province was called Therbasciland, a city famous for its desert and rustic mountains. Masnesia being a small country, there were very few schools over there. The most prestigious school in the country was the Woodrock International School.

15 years back, the school was just as normal as it was. Normal students, which consisted of a bunch of smart kids, athletes, brats and some dull students. But, there were only 2 students in the whole school who were beyond these categories, they were smart, imaginative, competitive, hard working and the list goes on and on. They were always destined to do something big.

One of them was a boy with black eyes with shades of brown and with a slightly light complex. He was tall and fit. He used to always sit with his blazer on his school uniform and answer questions as if he was the person who discovered those formulas and ideas. He was a usual teen with just three years for his high school to end.

He was a man of inquisitiveness and aspiration to do things which others haven't and couldn't even think of doing. He did have a bit of snobbishness in him and never showed any apprehension or anxiety on his face. He would react to situations as if he never gets frightened and is never going to lose any gamble he takes. He doesn't believe in failures, maybe that's why he never fails. Nor does he believe in success, feeling that anything he had achieved is just too small, maybe small for him.

He was an athlete who could even run like a tracer bullet on water. He was the person almost everyone in class wanted to be like, he was considered the champion by the majority. He would give you the answer for all the why's and what's. He was the man, he was Adro Whyson.

Adro never believed that there was someone as competitive as him because he found the whole class cheering and supporting him and always in his side. But he never used to flaunt about it.

But just like his class, he also ignored one peer of his. That one peer was boycotted for every single activity in class; He never spoke to or mingled with anyone. He had no friends, in other words he was a loner. He was as intelligent and competitive as Adro. He was always placed at the back with his skinny body lying towards the wall.

He never spoke to anyone nor opened his

mouth in class. He used to do everything on his own and never asked for help. He was the only person who used to score as much as Adro but never was recognised. In fact, he was the hidden rival of Adro Whyson.

He was an active person in nature, but why was that he had no friends? Why did he never associate himself with the class? Why was he the best in everything except for sports. He never came for sports classes nor did the teacher ever inquire about his absence. The answer to this all lies in one word, this disorder was so dangerous that it could affect him so badly and also be fatal. It was called Haemophilia.

This disorder of his was known by the entire faculty in the school, except for his friends. Due to which his parents had ordered the faculty to keep him away from the whole class, just to avoid any mishaps.

Due to the seclusion, his silence and loneliness has become venom in him. His one and only enemy was the person who used to be the most popular person in class. He was the lone enemy of Adro Whyson. He was known to the world as Hobad Doughnauts.

Hobad was very cold towards Adro because Adro was the person bagging the lime light while Hobad was just placed at the corner.

One day when everyone was cheering Adro as he won the school's ultimate football cup by being the highest goal scorer. All were lost in the happiness of the victory of the class's favourite while the loner of the class was left behind.

Inside him, his blood was boiling way beyond the boiling point as his anger would also lead to the evaporation of his blood. His anger was getting uncontrollable and he felt like giving punching eveyone, but he couldn't.

"Adro is the best!!" One shouted from the crowd. "No one can compete with him." exclaimed another one. Suddenly everyone started to shout, "He is the one and only, Adro Whyson!!"

Everyone was going crazy while a deep voice came from the back. A voice no one had ever heard. "Stop! He is not the best. He isn't even a competitor. I am better, in fact the best" Shouted Hobad with the deepest and loudest of voice ever heard.

Hobad got out of his reserved seat and walked towards the group and said, "You never noticed me, but I am better than all of you and even better than this Adro, who you put on your shoulders." Hobad said with a smirk on his face. He was releasing all his anger and hatred he had against the class with this opportunity.

Others started to oppose him while Adro was just silently looking at everything which was taking place and was not bothered to react to Hobad's statement. Hobad closed his fist and slaped a student who was supporting Adro. The class erupted in anger and pounced on Hobad to attack him. Hobad then spotted a pencil with a sharp led, he grabbed the pencil and held it still at his eye level in front of everyone.

They all moved a step behind, thinking that Hobad is going to scratch them with the pencil, but things turn out different. Hobad instead scratches himself and blood started oozing out of the small scratch in full flow.

"Someone help!" He cried for help. "aagh, that hurts. Somebody help me?" Hearing Hobad's voice, teachers came running towards Hobad's class to his rescue.

Students were surprised to witness Hobad bleeding by such a small scratch and teachers sprinting towards for him where as they never even bothered if someone had fractured themselves.

"What happened to you Hobad?" Mr. Hodreks asked worryingly. "Look at this Sir, I am bleeding. This pain is unbearable." He cried. Mr. Hodreks, was the head of department. His position was called as a supervisor in the school.

He ordered the support staff to call the ambulance and admit Hobad to the hospital. "Tell me Hobad?" The supervisor asked gently, "Don't feel scared. Tell me." Hobad then started to take deep breaths spoke with his voice trembling in fear. "Sir, I was pushed and scratched using a pencil by Adro." He said, pointing his fingers towards Adro.

Everyone was shocked to hear this. The pupils in the class were surprised to hear Hobad directly blame Adro when Hobad was an alien to Adro. The supervisor was also stunned to hear Adro do something obnoxious like this.

"Adro! Come to my cabin right now." He ordered. Adro was called in and was interrogated about the incident.

Mr. Hodrex was not ready to listen to Adro and stopped him, "Look Adro. I know you are one of the best students in the school, in fact the best. But I am sorry to say that if you are going to harm a person suffering from haemophilia like this, then you will be fired." Adro was shocked rather than surprised to hear this.

He replied, "What? Haemophilia? But we never knew about this and he harmed himself Sir."

"Be quiet and go back to your class. I do not want to hear anything from you." Adro was stopped by Mr. Hodrex and was sent back to the class.

As Adro was leaving the cabin, he heard Mr. Hodrex call up someone in urgent. "Hello, May I speak to Mr. Rickman Doughnauts." He asked and got his line. "Hello Sir, I am the supervisor of your son, Hobad doughnauts.

I am sorry for the inconvenience caused by one of our pupils in the school and we will see that it never happens again." He rapped up in full speed with his voice portraying fear and finished his talk with the tycoon. "Oh! Hobad is the son of the founder and CEO of Banana Electronics? I never knew that. Should be careful then." Adro said to himself as he left the room.

Now he had received something. An invitation to enter the war. The war against Hobad, a new enemy not just to Adro but to the whole world.

This was the beginning of the war between the two.

Things don't change !

* * *

11 years have gone by and things have just changed. Passing out of the Wodrock High School, in the same school in which Adro had done his schooling. He was just a year senior to me but it was fun and exciting being a bus friend of his.

After school, he chose to pursue his career in Computer science and did Masters and PhD in Computer science from Carnegie Melon University. He had published hundreds of research papers and had won acclaim. He was in a different world; he was going in a pace no one could even get close to it. He was regarded the master of Computer Science.

Adro also liked medicine, just because he always had the yearning to know why medicines react differently in different situations. But knowing what his strengths are, he chose to restrain himself which he was perfect at.

In the meantime, Hobad had overtaken Banana Electronics and unfortunately for Hobad, the markets were not in his favour and Hobad demanded something new from his employees.

Hobad was never satisfied with anything; in fact he became more and more restless as days went by. He was in search of someone who had the solution for his disorder. He wanted absolute immunity from haemophilia and he did not get it. Nor did he get the perfect gadget, which he could showcase to the world.

Every quarter, his assigned senior management discussed about the downfall of the company. "Look Hobad, coming at the end of Q2, There is a decline of 35.6% in our profit. In ten years, we have drastically gone down from the top 3 to the top 50." discussed Mr. Brown, who had been working for Banana for the past 20 years. "Our company is going down and will go down if we continue to do nothing. I feel that we can do nothing. This company is not doing well."

Hobad was tired of listening to his absurd speech. Hobad switched on his MacBook and was busy typing something on his laptop. Looking at Hobad's ignorance, Mr. Brown asked, "Are you listening to me. What are you going to do? If you are just going to do something on your computer and not focus on our company, then you are not fit to be in this post."

Hobad was going on typing and after a second of silence, he tapped his mouse and said, "Sorry Brown, I was just clearing some menace." Before he could complete his statement, a notification popped out on Brown's phone. Brown still continued to talk, but then he was stopped by Hobad. "Mr. Brown, it would be better if you could pause for a second and have a look at your notification." He said.

Brown took out his phone to have a look at his mail. As Brown started to read the mail, Brown was furious. "Why did you fire me? I have been working here for 20 years." He shouted. "You might be working for 20 years, but you called a MacBook a computer." A disgusted Hobad stated.

"Go home and relax and practice speaking with pauses."

"But I accidentally said computer, why did you have to fire me for that."

"Mistakes aren't accepted in my company Brown. I don't accept flaws and people who repent for this"

Hearing this, a speechless Brown left the meeting room with shame and disgust in his face. "Thank you very much guys for this wonderful presentation." Hobad remarked sarcastically. "If I observe the same result again, then I am afraid that you all will turn into today's Brown. You guys can now leave." He ordered and everyone left the room in seconds.

Hobad had a look at the newspaper which was on the desk. The headlines read, "He is the Genius. He is Adro Whyson." That article mentioned everything about Whyson and his growth. Hobad was now even furious. Every time he thought about Adro, it reminded him about his disorder.

He then recalled a scientist he had met, He was intelligent and also imaginative and in fact he was a chemist who had proposed to Hobad to help him anytime. Hobad took out his visiting card from his desk and rang a call from his landline. "Hello. Is it Dr. Tag?" He asked. "Yes. It's him." He replied in a 'pun intended' way. "It's nice to receive your call Mr. Doughnauts." He replied with a British accent. "I have an offer which you can't refuse." Hobad said. "Oh really!" Dr. Tag exclaimed. "I hope it's something interesting and not boring like programming your billion dollar vault or creating an advanced firewall system."

"Of course it's not like that" Hobad replied with a laugh. "This is going to be tough, rather too tough and I believe all your knowledge shall be implemented."

"Come on my friend!" Tag replied. "I am already equipped". "Then meet me in my office at eight in the morning." Hobad replied with a smile which was felt by Tag.

Hobad then hung the line and took a deep breath as he was relaxed that there was someone willing to take up the initiative to cure him. Hobad knew that as Tag was a known person to his father, Tag was aware of Hobad's disorder and would bring a great solution for this. He then stared at Adro's article in the paper and murmured, "Adro, I will surpass you." releasing all his anger on that statement. "Just wait and watch."

Nameless

* * *

Adro had a name made for himself. He had created gadgets and his discoveries had changed the world. He was the young sensation, who was changing the world at such a young age and was continuing to clinch up to his achievement.

I was lucky to get his phone number and meet him too. Being somewhat a known friend of his, Adro allowed me to come to his lab and have a look at his new creation.

Unsurprisingly, Adro had located his lab at the outskirts of Masnesia city. An area which had nothing but just barren land filled with sand, located en route Therbasciland from Masnesia city.

This was not amusing for me as I felt that just like other laboratories mentioned in movies and books, this too would be somewhere outside the main city. But in Masnesia, everything was near and reachable and this too was the same.

Just 20 kilometres away was a colossal 15 story building which stood tall as an office for a company. Co-incidentally, Hobad's enemy was situated close to him. But this lab of Adro's was never noticed by Hobad nor did Adro know that he had a devil just 20 kilometers away from his working place.

After an hour journey from home, at last I reached his lab. It was in a hemispherical shape surrounded by barren land and just two parking sheds. I parked my Ford Explorer below the empty shed as the other one was already filled by a red colour Mercedes SLS AMG.

When I got into the lab, it completely took me to a new world. With the blue lights switched on and one fourth of the lab was covered with glass, giving you the view of the highway of Masnesia City.

"Hello Eprun, how are you?" rushed Adro Whyson with his screw driver in his hand as he was fixing a machine. This machine was in the shape of a vending machine but had been installed with cameras and sensors on the border of the machine. This system was about 3 meters high and having a meter width and length.

"Hello Whyson!" I exclaimed. "What's going on?" I asked again. "Oh nothing much Eprun, I am just working on my new invention." He said in casual manner, making it look as if anyone could do so. He ran from the docking station of the machine to his table, taking his pliers in his hands from the plastic table and chopping down some wires inside the machine. "Can you brief me on what this is?" I asked but there was still no reply from Adro.

Before I could complete, Adro got up from his place and got to the table and passed me some papers to me. It did take me a while to understand his plan. His plan raised my eyebrows as I thought this would be impossible. "Seriously Adro?" I asked in astonishment and he just replied with a smile and again continued with his work.

"These descriptions on the papers do sound bizarre, but could you just brief me on your venture?" I asked. Adro was busy tapping several buttons and observing the response of the machine. After a minute, without me asking him again, He replied, "Sorry Eprun that you had to wait for my answer for a very long time. This machine has been created to merge to evolving factors."

"I haven't given any name to this machine yet but this gadget can now help and make you chose your own clothes you want and in half a minute, you would be wearing your desired clothes." He explained.

I was not convinced at the beginning but keeping in mind that he had done a PhD from one of the world's most coveted universities, it could be possible if he had said so. Adro asked me if I would want to be the first one to try it. I was overwhelmed as I did not have any words to say when I heard him give me the opportunity to try his masterpiece.

I stood in front of the huge cubical machine with its cameras scanning me and I had to turn give it a 360 degree view. On the side of the machine was a small screen that gave me the option to choose the clothes I wanted to wear. The best part was that I could also virtually make my own clothes and get it to the real world.

I was blank at that stage and did not have anything in mind nor was I suggested by Adro. I decided to play safe and just for name sake, chose an Adidas T-shirt and shorts with a puma shoes. It did sound ridiculous but the flaw in me was that I never could think on my feet and needed a long time to buffer and then implement my points.

The machine accepted the command and all of a sudden, started to shake vigorously. I did not have a good feeling though but Adro was standing behind, watching me with a calm and composed attitude, showing as if he never knew there is something called tension, success and failure. "Please stand still" Commanded a robotic voice, that came from the speakers of the machine and echoed throughout the lab.

From the front screen, where my image was to be seen with my present polo T-shirt and my Wrangler jeans, a group of red rays were emitted from the screen. Those rays were so powerful that it completely hindered by vision for a moment and I could see nothing.

As soon as I gained sight, I saw myself completely different. I was the same Eprun, but the clothes were different. My desired Blue coloured Adidas T-shirt was glowing on the front screen of the machine, with my Fluorescent Green shorts and shoes, I was delighted to witness the masterpiece do the perfectionist's work.

I rubbed my eyes once, I rubbed it twice, I rubbed it thrice but still I couldn't believe my eyes. I looked down at my shoes and garments and see my clothes pop out of a digital machine.

"It looks good Ep!" Adro exclaimed. He just had a smile in his face, never referring, boasting or inquiring about his patent model. It was as if he knew it before that it will work. "Have any name for this device Ep?" He asked me. "I guess it would be great to call it 'The Changer'" I suggested.

Adro looked at his machine for a minute and then turned back towards me. He stood still staring at me as if he was going to utter something and he would tell it any time.

"You know what?" He stated. "I guess let's keep its name as nameless. No one would ever be so engrossed to know about the name." He said in a firm manner, keeping it clear that he wouldn't like anyone to intervene in his decision. He took out a microchip from the machine and handed it over to me stating, "This microchip should be kept safe by you. If not, then don't ask me where your previous attire is."

Adro said, making his way out to see me off. I started to laugh as I have heard people store their clothes in wardrobes, suitcases and backpacks but never had I heard someone store it in a microchip. It did sound weird and prudent, comparing it for the needs of today's world.

I had to go out for my office work and left his laboratory. As I walked towards my car, I commented, "Nice car Adro. How is this car overall?" I asked. "Thanks Ep for your compliment. This car is going through some modifications and it would be ready in a week. For now, I catch the cab to go back home."

"What changes do you mean Adro? Are you going to make this fly?" I asked sarcastically. "You never know Eprun." He replied, "You may never know."

The Tagoplasm

❄ ❄ ❄

Dr. Tag was on time. He was waiting outside Hobad's cabin with a huge file, containing dozens of papers about his research and ideas. He was excited and anxious to meet Hobad. Dr. Tag knew very well that Hobad was a person who would not keep his work on top of his priority list and first comes his health and his well being.

In the mean time, Hobad was surfing through the net to find out more on his disorder and how it could be rectified. Researches have shown that haemophilia could only be mitigated by gene therapy but not fully cure it. Hobad then rubbed his hands to keep himself warm from the tension going through his mind and called up the receptionist to send Tag to his room.

"Dr. Tag, Mr. Doughnauts would like to meet you now." The receptionist informed. Dr. Tag's eagerness to portray his idea was making him rush to the CEO's cabin.

As soon as he entered, Hobad never got up to respect the well learned man, who was a very close person to Rickman Doughnauts and suggested him with mind-boggling ideas. But Dr. Tag never ever noticed if Hobad was not willing to listen or know about anything else, except the fact if he can be cured or not.

"Hello Hobad. Today I am going to explain about my idea..." Before the doctor could complete, Hobad asked his straight forwardly, " Can you cure my disorder or not?" Hobad was also expecting a straight answer and it was a confident 'yes' form Dr. Tag.

"Okay then…" Hobad commanded, "You can go on with your explanation." Hobad had given him the thumbs up signal to explain his vision and how it was to work.

He did take 2 hours to explain the whole process and also clear the predicament in Hobad's mind. Dr. Tag called this state of the art technology of his as the Tagoplasm. Tagoplasm was an electronic biochemical solution that was to be injected into the patient.

How this solution would work is that it would send in a small amount of chemical into the inner organs, to keep it stiff and prevent it from bleeding. These chemicals would then settle over there. The rest would stay on top of the skin as an extra layer of coating on the body, protecting it from bleeding due to a physical contact with any sharp and injurious substance.

Dr. Tag knew that even though Hobad would be satisfied with this, he would be expecting for something more. So he decided that in addition with this feature, this solution could protect the person's outer body from anything, anywhere. It can be a small scratch by a nail or a nuclear bomb, any harm can be sustained by this particular person injecting this solution in him and then he would feel no pain, no harm.

Also, this was termed by him as an electronic device and while narrating about Tagoplasm, he also mentioned that this gadget will have a firewall system build for this to prevent any hacking or the switching off of the advanced processing system which was placed in a tropical island. Much beyond the vision of anyone, and anyone attempting to destroy the island would fail. What Dr. Tag claims is the island and the room in which it is located is bomb-proof and can't be destroyed by any natural disaster.

The firewall created was inaccessible by anyone and could only be deactivated only with the thumb impression of Dr. Tag. Making it clear that as a loyal scientist, Hobad can trust Dr. Tag.

Dr. Tag was about to turn Hobad from a physically weak individual to a mentally, physically and socially super strong person.

Hobad Doughnauts was delighted to hear this and approved this project right at once. He took out his cheque book, which was lying on his table and in quick pace singed off a cheque, tore it off and handed it over to Dr. Tag. "What????" Dr. Tag asked with glee as his eyes were wide open, as if it would pop out. "I never expected to get 10 Million Masnesian Dollars for this though!" He exclaimed.

Hobad got up from his seat and kept his hand on Dr. Tag's shoulders and patted, saying, "Doc, don't underestimate your potential."

"You have done me a commendable favour by bringing me the greatest solution ever to my worst problem. But when you come to know, it will be so surprising that you won't be able to tell anything." Hobad commended with a smile in his face, knowing for sure that Dr. Tag or anybody on earth could and never would be able to guess what Hobad would do next.

The Test(S)

* * *

As Hobad had given the thumbs up to Dr. Tag to proceed on his work, Adro Whyson too was on the verge to do something different.

Through what I knew, Whyson was a person who always wanted to do something really unique and would keep racking up his brain to come up with something different. After succeeding in his nameless invention and also giving me a new pair of clothes, 25 days had gone since I ever spoke to Adro. Neither did he pick up my calls nor replied to my messages. It was as if, he had isolated himself. But why did he isolate himself? Where was he now? I had no idea about it.

Adro used to socialise with people, but would also know when to refrain from wasting his time on futile exercises such as chatting for hours and hours. So I felt it would be better to leave things as it is.

A month and a half after the meeting, a private aircraft makes a landing into one of the private islands located in the tropical region of Africa. Out of the boeing 777 came Hobad, wearing a white T-shirt with his sunglasses on and nothing with him except for his phone and a deodorant in his pocket. He was greeted by Dr. Tag, who was waiting for him with his Land Rover LR 4, keeping his engine switched on.

"Welcome Hobad." Dr. Tag said walking towards his important customer. "Good Morning Doc." Hobad replied, shaking hands with Dr. Tag. "So are you ready with your..." before Hobad could complete, Dr. Tag went on to fill in the blanks, "Yes Hobad, It's all ready. Now I am just waiting for you to try it.

Hobad gave an enthusiastic smile and was escorted by Dr. Tag and got inside the Land Rover and got off from the private airfield. "You must be hungry?" Dr. Tag asked. "I'm good." Hobad replied, texting something on his phone. He then took a moment to have a look at the island and was mesmerised at the scenic landscape. The island was of course surrounded by water and had mountains flooded with flora and fauna, standing tall facing the waters. In other words, it was a paradise

"So sad." Hobad replied with a sigh. "Patients don't often get such an amazing hospital to visit." passing a sarcastic comment. This comment evoked laughter in the driver and Dr. Tag who was sitting next to the driver.

The SUV was then heading towards a bridge. That bridge did take them a very long way, before they could reach another island. But this island was too small. In fact there was nothing except for rocks and sands and just a very small cottage.

Hobad was silent, keeping his phone inside his pocket and observing his trip very carefully. As soon as they reached, the SUV entered the cottage as the doors of the cottage were wide opened for the

SUV to get inside.

As soon as they entered the cottage, Dr. Tag took out his phone and opened an app. He was looking at it for a very long time he said, "Move 3 inches back." He commanded and it was done according to his command.

"Perfect then" Dr. Tag stated and clicked the button on his phone and then sat back with a relaxed face and said, "Go on"

The car suddenly started to go down. It was as if a lift was pulling it downwards. After 10 seconds, the car had landed down to a surface, but this seemed like a surface of a tunnel. Then all of a sudden, street lights started to flash on, giving the dark pathway some brightness.

This did seem like a 4D spaced cottage, but of course it was not. The car then went on going forward. The trip did look endless as they were moving on and on. As they were going on, instantly the chauffer drifted towards the right.

After a while, the car came to a haul and Dr. Tag and Hobad got down from the car. In front of them was huge wall, blocking the path of all of them. Dr. Tag entered the password on the system which was placed at the corner of the wall.

The system accepted the password and then granted access to the room beyond sight. The wall slowly started to repel from each other from the middle, and then the miracle was in front of them, the room beyond sight. The room beyond sight was truly upto it's name. It was a room from which the underwater marine life could be observed. It provided a 270 degree view of the Indian Ocean, which strechted towards parts of Africa.

"Welcome to Cellnesia, Hobad" Welcomed Dr. Tag with glee. "This is my office, here is where all my ideas come to life and this is the place from where you will be going out with a new life.

"Oh yes Doc! So when will we start?"

"We will start the process right now. Sit down on that chair." Stated Dr. Tag, pointing towards the reclined chair, normally used in hospitals to take a blood test.

Hobad sat there, facing a huge LCD screen which was attached on the wall. The screen had some systems connected to it and a cable, which was about 5 meters long, close to the radius of the room, ran all the way from the connected systems to Hobad's chair.

"Could you please rest yourself on the chair." Requested Dr. Tag, who was typing some codes on his laptop, which was wirelessly connected to the colossal system.

As soon as Dr. Tag finished typing, he kept the laptop on a table which was on the other side of the room and walked towards Hobad. He took out a syringe, which was about 5 inches big and connected it to the cable.

The chemical, which was greyish in colour started to produce small bubbles for about a minute. "These are the chemicals, which are flowing straight from the hardware systems placed." Dr. Tag informed Hobad. "This is the Tagoplasm, which is now going to protect your body and no one can mitigate the effect of this chemical, unless I deactivate it using my fingerprints."

As Dr. Tag brought the syringe close to Hobad, Hobad asked, "Why can't my fingerprints be used to safeguard this?" Dr. Tag replied with an arrogant smile on his face stating that the information present in the system are highly confidential and no one would ever come to know that it was set by Dr. Tag. Even if anyone comes to know about this system, he might attack you or try to catch hold of you but never will they know that Dr. Tag can only control everything.

Hobad was not convinced as he felt that Dr. Tag was boasting about his breakthrough and was beating around the bush to reveal the reason behind Dr. Tag's control over Hobad's shield. But Hobad just gave a smile and didn't allow his doubts to be shown in his attitude.

Dr. Tag clicked a small button which was present on the syringe. As soon as he clicked it, Dr. Tag pierced it into Hobad's right arm. A loud scream erupted from Hobad as soon as he was injected. All of a sudden, the LCD also came to life and started to show some images, which looked like inside the human blood vessels.

Hobad couldn't move his hands then, after a while he wasn't even able to move his legs. In no time, his whole body got stiff, only his eyeballs moving left and right.

At this stage, the Tagoplasm was trying to make Hobad's body strong and stiff. The chemicals were on their verge to make Hobad's cells and body organs strong and powerful. After a couple of minutes, Hobad regained his control over his body.

It was the longest two minutes of his life, but these two minutes had actually changes his life. Now, his inner and outer organs were protected by the Tagoplasm. Even a nuclear bomb could do nothing to Hobad and he could actually survive from all the radiation.

Hobad got up from the chair and stood at the same position for a minute, shaking his hands and legs, acknowledging himself that now he is the most powerful man on Earth. His self confidence was now at the peak. He was now too energetic to do anything. His happiness had no bounds.

"Happy Hobad?" Asked Dr. Tag, who was on the systems now connected to his laptop. He was collecting all the details of his work. "Yeah! I am good. This is the best moment ever!" He exclaimed. "But tell me doc?" Hobad asked, "Why can't you save my fingerprints on the system? I am not foolish enough to deactivate your tagoplasm?" He commented.

"Look Hobad." Dr. Tag said. "You might not be foolish to do that, but people around you can easily fool you though." Dr. Tag stated with a sarcastic smile on his face, teasing about Hobad's association with people and his weakness. Hobad could accept anything, except for anyone highlighting his weakness or being better than him.

From the lab to the airfield, Hobad couldn't stop himself from not thinking about Dr. Tag's discourteous behaviour towards Hobad. Hobad felt that he had let him and his status down by asking someone for help and that's why Dr. Tag was flaunting about his security and control over things.

When Hobad was about to get into the plane, Dr. Tag inquired, "How are you feeling Hobad?" He asked. Knowing that Dr. Tag was almost 20 years older to him, he knew that a bad remark would upset him and maybe in anger, he might deactivate the Tagoplasm.

"Wow!" He exclaimed, "I only have this much to say." He lied to Dr. Tag, controlling his anger. "Come to my office next week." He requested. "I want to congratulate you in front of my employees."

Dr. Tag gave a big smile to his request. "This is an offer I can't refuse." He laughed.

The Attraction

* * *

Adro Whyson has not been in touch with me for about one and a half months. I felt that I needed to pay a visit to his lab, just to check out what's been created over there.

So I took my car and drove towards his lab to explore about Whyson. I left for Adro's lab at 10 AM in the morning. Being a Friday, traffic was expected en route to Adro's lab. It took me 2 hours to reach his location and another 15 minutes to navigate his laboratory.

As I reached there, I immediately shot a glance towards his car shed and spotted a different car taking the place of the Mercedes Benz SLS AMG. There stood a Black Audi S4. I parked my car on under the shed and immediately approached the security system which could only grant me access to get into the lab only if I could type the password.

It was an alpha-numerical password and I tried to recall the password given to me by Adro. I tried hard to remember but I couldn't. I then decided to try my luck and randomly pressed two keys which were 1and 8 and then the OK button. Surprisingly, it worked and I could get into his lab.

When I got in, I noticed Adro was busy on his equipments and didn't even notice that I had got in. "Hello Mr. Adro" I greeted. Adro was shocked to hear me, maybe because he hadn't heard from anyone in the past 45 days. "Oh hello Eprun." He replied. "Your visit is totally unexpected."

"I know that Adro. You have not socialized with anyone for the past 45 days." I said. "You are wrong Eprun." He replied "Get your stats right. I haven't spoken to anyone or participated in any events for the past 48 days and 13 hours. Don't give me any estimation." He grinned.

"What's the matter Adro?" I asked. "Why are you so angry?" "I am just not getting it right." He replied. "By the way, how did you get into my lab?" He asked.

"I just typed the password." I replied. Adro stared at me for a couple of seconds and said, "I had changed the password 43 days ago to avoid such nuisance." adjusting something on the smart watch on his hand.

"I actually just guessed the password. I never knew it though." I replied. "Oh! So I guess your luck has now got unlucky for me." He stated.

Adro was now glued on the smart watch on his hand. He then placed it on the table next to him. On that table was a glass cup placed, which was partially filled with water. Adro wore a pair of dark blue gloves, which were a bit stiff. He wore the smart watch on his left wrist and switched on the watch.

It looked like a watch which was not only smart but was too intelligent. Adro clicked on a feature on his watch called 'The Attractor'. I seriously had no idea what that attractor was going to do nor did I ever think of asking Adro about what it was about. I just quietly observed what he was doing.

The watch took some time to load and then Adro took his right palm and opened it, towards the glass. The watch spoke out loud, "3, 2, 1 and, GO!" Adro was now still, only focusing on glass. The glass started to shake a bit. Then, this vibration was even more intense and then it started to shake even more vigorously. We all were quiet as Adro started to move his hand left and right. The glass slowly started to move towards Adro.

It took a couple of minutes for the glass to barely move 2 centimetres. As Adro was trying to bring the glass closer to him, he lost control over the glass, causing the glass to move away from Adro. Adro still tried to bring the glass come towards him by shaking his hands back and forth. But unfortunately, due to the vigorous shaking of the glass, the glass and the water inside it exploded. Scattering the glass pieces and drops of water all over the lab.

"Oh no!" cried Adro. "I Just got control of it and lost it again." He said, being surprised by the result of his test. "But I have never lost and will not lose in this too." A determined Adro stated. "I have already won. I just need to learn to control this."

After talking to himself aloud, he started at me, as if I had done something wrong. "What??" I asked. "I didn't do anything." I said. Adro replied to this with a smile and said, "Okay then. Let me take a break." He said. "Its ages since I've gone back home."

As we left the lab, I asked, "So what is that smart watch all about." Adro looked at me for 3 seconds and I asked, "Now what have I done?"

"Nothing bad." He laughed and took out the watch from his hand. "This watch is called the 'Ion-ovalent watch'. This watch has been designed to suit my purposes and needs."

"Excellent!" I said, "What are the amazing features in the watch?" I asked. "Do you have any description about this project of yours?"

Adro was just walking towards his Audi and turned back at me and said, "No! You will find it out at the right time" I then asked, "Can you explain about your project in brief." Adro then paused for a moment, "It shows the time." He winked.

The next question I had was to ask him about his Merc which was not to be seen, but felt that I would be expecting a similar type of answer for this, and left it.

As Adro and Eprun, finished their talks and left the lab. There was one man who was observing their meet through his binoculars. "Oh, as my enemy gets closer and closer, I get stronger." Murmured Hobad, sitting inside his Lexus ES 350. "One is just going to last for another 2 days while the big fish is just 20 Kilometres away from my office."

"Don't worry." He was talking to himself, "Even your end isn't too far away." Hobad grinned, having a last peek at Adro and then changing his gears from parking to drive and moved away from the point.

On my finger tips

✻ ✻ ✻

2 days later, Hobad drives his Lexus towards the Masnesia international Airport to pick up Dr. Tag.

Hobad was waiting for Dr. Tag, wearing a black suit and his shades on. He was anxious to meet Dr. Tag, nothing else but he had given a list to Dr. Tag, which he wanted badly. He felt that Dr. Tag was the best person he knew who could turn absurd ideas into reality.

As Dr. Tag was getting his baggage scanned, in the mean time Hobad was busy checking his stock market. As Dr. Tag came out, Hobad was there to receive him.

"Hello Dr. Tag." Hobad welcomed him, shaking hands with him. "Have you brought the stuff I needed?" He asked. "Yes Hobad!" Dr. Tag replied with a glee. "It's the best product from the best dealer." He flaunted.

Hobad nodded his head in agreement and then was followed by Dr. Tag to his golden coloured Lexus.

"Nice car Hobad." remarked Dr. Tag. "Perfectly camouflages with the desert." He added. "Sure it might." Hobad replied. "And we might get too late if you don't get inside."

Dr. Tag got into the car and Hobad zipped off from the airport. "Didn't you hire a driver?" Dr. Tag asked. "Yeah I could, but I spent all on you my friend." He stated, keeping Dr. Tag mum with the remark.

"Now open your suitcase and please show me what you have got for me." Hobad pleaded. "Okay then." Dr. Tag unlocked his case, and there it was, just what the master ordered, two bombs. These bombs could have been brought from anywhere but little did Dr. Tag know why he was asked to make them.

"Okay Doc." Hobad said, "We are nearing the position." Hobad drove towards Adro's Lab. As soon as he reached there, he looked at the lab with a smile. A smile, that was evident on Hobad's face that he was going to vanquish his enemy's base. He was going to declare war on Adro and perhaps the biggest war ever between two people. It wasn't between two countries, states or communities. It was the war between Hobad Doughnauts and Adro Whyson.

Hobad glanced at the security system and immediately ordered, "Doctor, hack the system."

"As you wish master." Dr. Tag replied, as usual with a pinch of sarcasm in his say and approached the pass code system. Dr. Tag took out feature phone from the pocket of his jacket. He switched on his phone and started to type something. As he was typing, he read it aloud, "QFJ238048#" and pressed the dial key.

He then brought the phone close to the pass code, and suddenly the locks of the lab opened. Dr. Tag pulled the handle to check if it worked or not, and as expected by Dr. Tag, the door invited them into the world of Adro Whyson's creation.

The whole lab was filled with gadgets, wires and papers. The two of them were very careful on the steps they took and also had a look around the lab. As Doughnauts was going around the lab, he got his eyes on a bunch of papers kept in a transparent file on a wooden table.

Just about 5 meters next to the wooded table was another one, this time made out of plastic, and with pieces of glass scattered and water spilled around it. Hobad was going through the files of the paper while Dr. Tag was searching for the best area to place the bomb. Hobad took out each and every paper out of the file and read each and every word, "Nameless it is." He murmured. "A machine that can change a person's outfit in a flash?" He was puzzled by this unique idea.

He turned back and saw the colossal machine, whose wires were plugged into a socket. "So this is the nameless." He said. "That's a great indeed."

As Hobad turned back to look at the other papers, the water on the floor caused Hobad to slip and fall down on the floor. As he fell down, a sharp piece of glass scratched him on his left hand. Hobad was terrified for a second, expecting the blood to ooze out rapidly but then was surprised at not seeing a drop of blood drop from his body and also his scratch disappear. "Now that's perfect." He smiled looking at his hand. "But I feel sad for the creator of this." He continued.

Dr. Tag had also placed the spherical bomb

next to the electrical switch board, expecting that the blast would be more effective. "Are you done Hobad?" He asked, coming out of the switch board room and walked towards the tables. Hobad collected the sheets of paper and replied, "100 percent perfect. Shall we leave?"

"I am not fond of staying here Hobad." He replied back, leaving the lab. As they got inside the car, an inquisitive Hobad asked, "How did you get past the security with the bomb in your suitcase?" Dr. Tag feigned his question and just got into the car, making Hobad angrier and having the feel to decimate him. But he decided to keep up to his unfathomable personality in front of Dr. Tag.

Hobad reached the freeway, which was less than 200 meters away from the lab and stopped at the corner of the road. He looked back through the side mirror to check if no one had seen them leave.

"That is good then." He stated and moved on. As they were moving on, Hobad asked Dr. Tag to switch on his phone, which was connected to the bomb. "Dr. Tag..." He screamed, "Detonate the bomb."

Dr. Tag clicked the okay button and Adro's lab exploded into flames. The blast could be heard about to about 10 kilometres away from the point. Hobad then changed his lane and stopped for a minute at the right side of the road.

"Just give me a minute Dr. Tag." He requested the doctor and got out of the car with the papers about the machine. Hobad opened the boot of his car and took out a suitcase. The suitcase consisted of a pair of clothes, socks and new shoes. Hobad placed the papers inside the case gently and also removed his coat. He stuffed it inside his suitcase and closed the case and the boot.

As he closed the boot, he smiled as his happiness had no bounds. He quickly got back to the car and flew away.

"In another 10 minutes, Adro will reach his burnt lab and there we will catch the fish." He informed Dr. Tag.

For your eyes Only !!!

❄ ❄ ❄

Just as what Hobad had manipulated, Adro was on his way to the lab. Adro wasn't aware of the status of his lab and therefore was playing the song 'Beat it' on his music system.

He was just 3 kilometres away as he spotted black smoke erupting from a distance. Adro immediately switched off the music system, from where he was listening to the songs and was closely observing the location from where the smoke came. "Was there a car accident?" Adro asked himself. "But a car accident can't be as destructive as this." He started to wonder.

"There isn't any factory or any company at this range, then from where would this smoke be coming from?" As Adro was trying to figure out, he now reached closer and was devastated to see the state of his lab. He was rather agonised by the abomination of his lab, which he considered as his workshop to express, create, innovate ideas and discover more about himself.

He was miffed for the first time ever on something which was beyond his control. Just as Adro was getting engulfed in grief, something had hit the bumper of his Audi S4. This jerked Adro for a moment. Before he could turn towards the side mirror to have a look at the car behind, his left side mirror was destroyed by a 9mm bullet.

Adro then decided to turn back and have a look of the driver from his rear view screen as his rear view camera was also vanquished by the bump. One thing Adro realised that the driver didn't do it by mistake. He then turned back and saw the face of the CEO of Banana Electronics, sitting behind the wheel and also shooting the bullets.

The next bullet pierced through the rear view screen, shattering the glass screen and also making Adro's rear view blurred. "Thanks for the revulsion Hobad." A frustrated Adro stated, losing his cool and accelerated away from Hobad with great speed.

Adro knew that he was now chased by Hobad to take revenge of his fame and bonding with people while Hobad failed to do so. Adro was well aware that Hobad considered him as a sworn-in enemy and would never leave anything to keep Adro alive.

The chase was followed with a lot of sharp turns and drifts. Adro didn't have any weapons with him while Hobad was well prepared with his ammunitions.

Hobad now had only 4 bullets left with him and he had to use his resources carefully. He went on knocking Adro from behind. Hobad then drove a bit faster to get ahead of Adro. As soon as he got in front of the Audi, Hobad skid the car, making a 270 degree drift and also changed his gearbox to reverse and moved backwards.

Now being in front of Adro, he could now get a clear aim of Adro. Hobad set the speed to a 180 kilometres per hour and cliked the cruise control mode. He then opened the sun-roof of the car and got his head on the roof to get a perfect view of Adro and his car.

Hobad took an aim on the engine of Adro's car and pulled the triggers. An observant and clever Adro drifted towards the right, getting himself on to the edge of the barren land, which was at the side of the highway, filled with sand. Adro's drift made the sand rise in the air, creating a dusty view for Hobad to see Adro.

Adro then took no time to settle down and cruised forward, to escape from the claws of Hobad.

Hobad was disappointed with the aim. He then got inside the car, deactivated the cruise control mode, changed to drive mode and turned around and moved forward, chasing Adro.

It was 4 PM in the evening and sun was gradually setting down. Adro did try his best to get Hobad out of control by taking sudden turns and making unexpected drifts, but none of those tactics worked.

This chase now led them to a region filled with rustic mountains, providing a wonderful view of Therbasciland. Hobad was now left with only 2 bullets in his gun and invested all of them by aiming at the tyres of Adro's car, but this too was in vain. Hobad then threw away his gun in disappointment and continued to chase Adro.

This long and interesting car chase now had lead them climbing the tallest mountain in the island of Masnesia, the Mount Civics.

This chase continued on the 7.4 mile road towards the peak of the mountain. When Hobad tried to knock Adro off from the mountain by giving him some hard knocks. Adro swiftly changed lanes, making things tough for Hobad.

Adro knew that Hobad would never leave him unless he was executed by Hobad. Adro looked towards his car's cup holder and spotted his gloves placed over there.

He tried to control the car and simultaneously wear the gloves too. As he reached the peak, he was ready with his gloves worn on both his hands.

As the both of them reached the peak, it was the end of their nasty chase as there wasn't anywhere to go beyond this and the whole spot was safeguarded with barriers.

Now both the cars were still. Hobad was now delighted has he had got his enemy trapped. His enemy had nowhere to escape and had no option but to surrender to Hobad.

Adro had other plans. He removed his seatbelt and bent forward. Adro then held his steering wheel tight and his foot just on the accelerator.

Adro accelerated with the speedometer clocking at 200 kilometres per hour, just as the Audi was about to knock the barrier, Adro applied a sudden break. This break caused Adro to come forward due to the inertia of motion and as Adro was not wearing his seatbelt, there was nothing to break the flow, thus making Adro break through the screen and jump out of the barrier.

There was a minute of silence after Adro jumped out screaming. The car too couldn't resist going forward and also fell off from the cliff.

"Nothing can get perfect than this." He stated, opening the boot of his car through the driver's seat and doing a 180 degree drift. As he drifted the car, the suitcase in Hobad's car fell out and rolled on the platform.

"Dr. Tag, I thank you for this great invention but I am sorry that I can't save you now." He said.

He clicked a button which was next on his steering wheel and read out, 'Self Destruct.' He then looked at Dr. Tag and then said "Sorry mate, I do trust your product, but not you." Dr. Tag didn't understand what Hobad was trying to say but before he could, he was left burning.

The car exploded with huge flames being produced. It was confirmed that Dr. Tag was dead, but then came out a person whose body was covered with flames. His clothes were burning and his whole body too.

Hobad walked away from the burning car and got his hand on to the suitcase. Soon, his flames were getting mitigated and no pain was evident on Hobad's expression. Now his enemies were gone. No one could ever harm him or deactivate the Tagoplasm. He was now a one man army who could do anything on Earth.

To cover himself up again due to the flames, He had kept this suitcase ready. So he quickly got off the point unless someone spots him and become a twitter sensation and be called as the '#Flameman.'

Assuming to be dead, Adro was actually clinging himself to the mountain, sticking himself just below the cliff. At the right time, he was able to control his gadget and got things right.

The attractor, which was the main feature of his watch, could attract or get the person attracted to any object. It could either be a metal or a non metal. Using the Whyson logic, he was able to save his life by hanging himself to the mountain.

Adro then scanned the whole town and then spotted a desert, which was comparatively near to the road. In a jiffy, Adro was on to his desired location and landed by skidding on the sand dunes.

Just next to his landing point were a group of people who had set up a tent and were camping. They were baffled by seeing a man jump from space.

Adro just had a look at them, "Hello" He greeted, and walked away from that place right at once. As soon as he reached the road, He was now hunting for a cab.

Somehow, he got hold of a cab and got inside. "Could you take me to the Checks Town city centre in Masnesia city?" He asked.

The driver was surprised with the request and asked, "Sir, are you aware that this is a Therbasciland Taxi?"

"Yes I do. But just take me there at once," Adro demanded.

"Okay then" The driver said, "but the fare would cause a big dent in your pocket."

"Don't worry Sir." Adro replied, "I have a sewing machine back home."

It's all in the brain

* * *

Due to heavy traffic, it took two and a half hours for Adro to reach Checks Town. It was already half past nine, but the city was still lit up by enthusiastic people keeping up the fad in the capital.

Adro had reached the entrance of Checks Town city centre and now had no idea where to go. He immediately took out his phone and then paused for a moment, "Is it 234 or 244?" Adro was typing the phone number and was stuck at the last three digits. "Oh yeah!" He exclaimed, "I got it." He then typed the number and then clicked the dial key.

I was in my house, sitting idle and watching Tom and Jerry. As I walked towards my table to get some tortilla chips in my bowl, a sudden ring on my phone frightened me.

I walked towards the sofa, on which I had kept my phone. I glanced towards it and saw the number of Adro flashing. This was the most unusual thing to ever happen as neither does he call me nor picks up my calls.

"Hello Adro." I answered, "Hi Eprun, Could you please tell me where the building you are staying in located from Cheks Town city centre is?" He asked, sounding as if he was gasping for breath and was scurrying around.

"It's the third building from there." I said. "Thanks a lot." He replied back. Before I could start to ask my question, Adro had already hung the phone.

5 minutes later, 'Ting Tong'. Someone rang the bell of my apartment and I went towards the door hole to check who it was. I immediately identified the person and opened the door, "Welcome Adro! It's surprising to see you over here."

Adro didn't smile. He entered the house and asked, "Can I rest in your house this night?" He asked. "Sure." I replied. You can take the second room, which is seldom used and you can freshen up too." I said.

I had no problem if Adro took a break over here, but I wanted to know why he wanted to stay here. What was the reason behind him to rush towards my house when he dislikes asking help from others?

After he came out of his room, "Is there any problem Adro?" I asked. Adro ignored my question and asked for a cup of water. After drinking the water, he said, "You know Hobad right?" He asked, "He had burnt my Lab into flames." A dejected Adro said. "I also lost my car, due to which I couldn't go home."

"How did this all occur?" I asked. Adro took the kettle, in which the water was filled and poured it in his glass and swallowed it in one gulp. After which he narrated the whole incident.

"That's too bad though." I commented. "But at last your watch has started to work." This comment of mine was expected to encourage Adro, but instead he stared at me for a minute with an angry face, and then laughed in happiness, "That's one thing I can celebrate about." He claimed.

"Okay then Eprun, let me go to bed." Adro walked off.

"Don't you want to have something?" I asked.

"No, I just need rest. See you tomorrow."

The next day, I dropped Adro at his villa, at six in the morning. Adro was in his house for the next 2 weeks and resumed his same attitude towards me via phone that was to boycott my calls.

2 days after, Adro came to meet me again, but this time he was anxious. "Eprun" Screamed Adro. "Did you ever go through my file?" He asked. "Which file Adro?" I asked back.

Adro was agitated. He replied back with rage on his face, "I am talking about the file which talked about my machine Nameless."

"I never went through all the files." I said, "For the matter of fact, I understood nothing from that and remember nothing either."

"If you do not remember, then how did this take place?" Adro switched on the television and on the news headlines appeared Hobad and the nameless machine, which was now manufactured by Banana Electronics. It was called as the Banana Wardrobe.

On the television screen was Hobad's speech being telecast to the world. He was explaining about what the machine was, its benefits to the society and the world, and also claiming the idea of this master piece to be his.

Adro was devastated by this. He had some suspicion on me, feeling that I would had leaked the information to Hobad. But he also knew that Hobad never knew me.

He then sat on my sofa and thought for a moment and racked up his mind for 10 minutes on how this could happen. After sometime, he was sure that I was telling the truth and that Hobad would have conducted a sting operation to obtain this information. But his gut feeling said that I couldn't have leaked out anything.

"This.....this is ridiculous." Adro shouted. "He had been keeping an eye on me." He began scratching his head and was mad at Hobad and wondered how he got hold of it. "Is there any relation between the blast of my lab and the leakage of this information? As soon as I had spotted the lab burning into flames, he knocked my car immediately. Is he the one who was responsible for the state of my lab? What do I do now?"

Just as Adro was expressing his grief, he had a look of the highlights of Hobad's speech, which was played on television. As Hobad entered the stage, he took out the mike and shouted loud in enthusiasm, "This is going to change your lives folks!!!"

This line was going through the mind of Adro for a while; He closed his eyes and was thinking about the same sentence. After a while, he opened his eyes and turned towards me and said, "Don't call me unless I call you." Saying this, Adro exited my house.

Just as he reached the door, I asked, "Why is that so Adro?" I asked. Adro gave an arrogant smile and then replied to my question, "See Mr. Tapeboy," For the first time addressing by my surname, "It's all in the brains."

I never understood Adro and what he used to say as I was too soft in the head for him. But I realised that he had other plans for the villain, Hobad Doughnauts. But what could they be? How effective will it be? No one ever knew. Adro was now ready to reply back to him.

The pain

* * *

2 months passed by, and Banana Electronics has seen the best quarter of the year. Their 3rd quarter, which was Q3, has gotten them close to $23.5 billion as their revenue, which was their highest revenue in any quarter for Banana Electronics.

Economists all around the world quoted the Banana wardrobe to be a game changer into the electronics industry, as this company had fashion and electronics merged.

But what no one could ever think about was about the worst that was yet to come. Banana Electronics had never had any complains about the Wardrobe and all the customers gave this a thumbs up.

It was a fine sunny day, the clouds were clear and the sun was shining bright in pride. Hobad Doughnauts had reached his office on his new white coloured Maserati Ghibli. He surprised everyone in the office, coming in with a happy face.

He immediately called for a meeting with his employees in the board room. In the room, everyone was anxious and was filled with a sense of apprehension of why they were called all of a sudden.

Then came in Hobad, who entered the room with a new device in his hand. Everyone stood up to respect their CEO. Hobad sat down on his seat and also asked others to take a seat too.

"I thank you all for making this venture a success." He appreciated, "You guys have made this spark that came into my mind a reality." He added. "To keep our success going, I have come up with a new device to make things going our way."

Hobad placed the device on the table, the device resembled a tablet, but this tablet had two cameras in the front screen and one at the back.

"So let's start." He said and tapped the screen on the tablet. All of a sudden, a holographic image arose from the front screen camera, depicting the tablet.

"This is the Banana ITab" He informed, getting up from his seat and started to explain about this by walking around the boardroom. "This gadget is set to keep our streak going. This tablet is different from others." He said clicking the holographic tablet which was projected in the air.

Everyone were mesmerised to witness that a person could literally click on the holographic image and it would respond.

The ITab didn't have anything different, except of the fact that this has now provided the air with senses. A click in the air and the user could do, access or watch anything.

After Hobad finished explaining about the device, all the members in the room stood up and applauded him and his creative ideas. "Thank you once again." He smiled.

As he left the boardroom, he spotted his personal assistant running towards him. "Pause PA, what happened?" Hobad asked. Hobad always used to call his assistant as PA and never bothered to call him by his name.

"Sir, there is a big problem." The PA said, gasping for breath. "The wardrobe has a big technical fault." He added. "Stop bluffing" Hobad said. "What type of problem is it?"

"Sir, I have got nearly about 12,000 mails, complaining about the gadget. They claim that they do not get the desired clothes they wanted and in return, they never got their old ones back from the chip."

Hobad was never convinced. He scurried up to his cabin and switched on his laptop to have a glance at his mails.

He was tired to see all the mails having the same subject, 'Technical error'. All his branches, which were set in all corners of the world were receiving the same complain from all customers. But as Hobad was scrolling through the mails, one mail got his eyes glued on. This mail had a completely different subject.

'A gift for you', the title of the subject stated. Hobad didn't have some good feeling about that particular mail and immediately clicked on it.

The sender's name was mentioned as The Brains. The mail read out,

Dear Hobad,

I am sad to hear the major technical

fault from your Banana Wardrobe. But I can only tell you one thing, you may take it as an advice, don't try copying difficult stuffs. It doesn't suit you.

Kind Regards,

You may know me.'

Hobad's anger was uncontrollable. "Adro" He shouted loud. He banged his desk with full force, releasing out his anger on the desk and furious about the fact that he was still alive..

In just 5 hours, Banana Electronics stock started to crash. This was now international news. TV channels had decided to air this news for the next 2 days, unless they get anything different. Banana Electronics was placed in a catastrophes state.

In other words, it was a win-win situation for Adro. But how did this entire ruckus occur in the first place. A device that has had absolutely no complains and also got Banana electronics to the limelight. What was the move taken by Adro Whyson.

Sitting on the couch and just switching on the television, I couldn't get a news as surprising as this. I immediately picked up my phone to call Adro, but just as I was about to dial the call, the phone suddenly went blank. The phone suddenly started to switch on and again went back to sleep. I was agonised and tensed by this abrupt behaviour shown by my phone, I started to tap my screen vigorously. "I told you not to call me." Came a voice that came from the entrance. When I turned back, there he was standing with a huge piston on his left hand.

"Adro!" I was astonished to see him, with his sorrow vanished on his face. "Did you see the news?" I asked.

"I am the one who made the news." He stated. As usual, I never understood what he said indirectly and he also knew it. He then pointed the gun towards me, which had a container on top of it, filled with some type of fluorescent green liquid, which was bubbling on. "This has made the news Eprun."

"Due to this, all the Wardrobes have gone empty and even your phone has become useless." He said. "I didn't get you." I said, frustrating Adro by not understanding his statement.

"For people experiencing happiness by cheating or betraying, this is pain for them." He said, "Peeda, this is called. Let it be the most advanced system, this can ruin its reputation." In Hindi, Peeda meant pain and that's where he got the name for his creation.

"Hobad betrayed me; actually that's what he had been aspiring to do for the past 20 years but just 2 months it took for me to spoil his game." I never expected Adro to turn the tables this way because he always believes in following moral values and rules. I asked him about why he was doing this, he just replied with one statement, "Once you have a target, do whatever it takes till it's legal, moral and ethical." He said. "I never go the bad way, but can't be good to the bad." He said.

Peeda was also the reason why my phone also went mad. I asked him, "Now what do I do to my phone?"

"It's very simple." Adro replied, "Just buy a

new one."

"I won't be in Masnesia for some time." He said. "So don't tempt me to make you buy another phone." Adro walked away, informing me about this. I didn't dare to ask him why he would not be in this country." But I felt that it would be better not to ask another question because it was getting obvious that Adro wouldn't say anything straight.

Eprun and Junward were just in the middle of their journey when Eprun said, "After that, I never meet Adro. After his transformation as a criminal, I just didn't bother to call him up. But my gut feeling says that he wouldn't have been killed."

"Then what do you think would have happened to him?" Junward asked. "I don't know Junward?" Eprun said shaking his head stating physically that he was clueless. "I seriously don't have any idea" Eprun sat back on his seat and took a deep breath as the train was flashing through the lush green land, which served as entertainment for the passengers.

The....... liquid

* * *

Chennai International Airport-2014

The Air Masnesia, which was the national carrier for the country, had landed on a Wednesday night. Out of the flight exited Adro Whyson, with just a suitcase and his passport in his coat.

He had booked an air ticket to Chennai in economy class. Even though he could travel by Business, he decided to control his budget.

Adro had actually come to Chennai assuming that Hobad would now be searching for him and he felt Chennai to be the best place to escape. He left his gadgets and fame back in Dubai. He had even got himself a 2005 Nokia 6282; so that no one would guess or think that he's a big shot.

Adro decided to stay in Chennai for at least 3 months. He had taken a single bedroom townhouse for rent, which was located in the industrial region of Chennai.

As vehicles in India were also affordable, Adro decided to purchase a Tata Nano for himself, which was considered as the world's cheapest car.

As his needs were all arranged by an acquaintance of his, Adro walked towards the open parking area and spotted a man sitting on a chair, facing the cars parked.

Adro walked towards him and asked, "Excuse me" The man turned towards his right and saw Adro Whyson. The man took out his phone and had a look at a picture sent to him. "Yes, its him" He murmured and took out an envelope from his pocket, stood up and handed it over to Adro.

"Mr. Whyson, Welcome to India." He greeted. "The car is at the 5th from the left on the 8th row." He informed.

"How do I get to my accommodation?" He asked. "It's all in the map." He replied. He had an Indian accent but never struggled in the pronunciation of words. "Thank you, Sir." Adro thanked and got to the car.

He tore of the envelope gently and took out the key from it. Inside the envelope was a map which leads him to his house, "Okay then, this should be a fun drive?" He told to himself and unlocked the car and drove away from the airport.

Adro did have a pleasant time in India. He would either sit in the garden or enjoy the weather on the terrace. He would either go for a long drive or have a long nap. Everything was fine; everything was going good for him.

In just a blink of an eye, only a week was left for Adro to leave this place. He felt that it would be the right time to go back and resume work but in the other hand, he also felt like staying back and extending his holidays.

It was half past 11 in the night and Adro was just returning after having a heavy dinner. The whole city was sleeping at this time and Adro could find no one on the road. Neither was there any vehicle nor anyone walking. Adro started to feel creepy as he was never used to seeing a place be so silent and compared to Masnesia, where you would find cars bustling during midnight, Chennai was the complete opposite.

Adro was just 10 kilometres away from his house; the breaks of his car had all of a sudden stopped working. He neither could control the speed nor stop the car. Adro had completely lost control of the car. Just at that time, Adro was notching close to 80 kilometres an hour and was also climbing the bridge that was situated above the Hash Brown Lake. This Lake was not brown in colour though, but it wasn't a very well known lake. It had an area stretching only four square kilometres and having factories around it.

Adro tried turning the steering wheel of his car, but couldn't get it move in a straight direction. Adro was filled with fear and agitation.

At the end, the car went out of control and the car jumped out off the bridge. Adro screamed up to his throat but no one could ever listen to him.

The car made titanic splash and sank down the bed of the lake. In no time, water started to enter the car and Adro took a deep breath and removed the seat belt.

He had to immediately get out of the car and was searching for the handle to open the door. He couldn't see anything in the dark water and thus it was difficult for him to find out where the handle of the door was.

He could feel the cold water rising up to his shoulders while he pulls each and every object he could catch hold off. At last, just as the water level came up to his chin, he got hold of the handled and pulled it with full force. As he always used to keep his doors unlocked, things came out to be easy.

As he opened the door of the car, the cold water from outside splashed right onto him and swallowed the car in one gulp and the car was left sinking its way down.

Adro's vision was now blinded; he could see nothing but only knew that he had to swim up to the ground level. Just as he started to swim up, instantly, he felt something grab his legs and was pulling him down. It was like a type of force that was pulling him down and down. Adro tried to overcome the force, but all his efforts were in vain.

He was swinging his hands and shaking his legs, but he was just getting pulled by this unknown force. Adro was about to give up as he no longer could hold on to his breath. He felt that it would be impossible to overcome this attraction and decided to surrender himself.

Just as Adro gave up holding his breath, he observed something exceptional, just as he gave up holding his breath. As a follow up it was human tendency to also inhale some air and just as he left out his breath, the impossible took place.

Adro was able to breathe in back some oxygen. This lake had something magical, mystical in it. Adro looked down for a second to see what was pulling him down and observed something unusual glowing down.

The fluid present was something Adro had never seen. He bent down to collect the substance, which was very small in quantity.

The liquid was slimy in nature and changed its colour rapidly. For some time it was purple, then it changed its colour to green then pink, orange, red and so on, the liquid exhibited a variety of colours.

"This is unique." Adro told to himself in his mind. He felt that due to this substance, he was able to breathe under water without any technical assistance.

He tried to hold it by closing his fist, but it went on to slip out. He then caught it back and tried to insert it in his pants pocket, but still it found its way out.

He tried multiple ways to catch hold of it and keeping it with himself but nothing could make him grab it. Just behind him, Adro started to feel some waves knocking his back. It felt like sitting in a Jacuzzi but after some waves, the wave started to becomc ferocious.

Adro was expecting the wave to come at the same interval and hit him from behind. But the wave took a different direction and pushed him in the upward direction.

Adro had grabbed the slimy liquid as the ferocious wave was pushing him up to the ground. Adro was piercing through the water in the upward direction with his body uncontrollable.

The wave was so strong that Adro couldn't get out of it. Adro was approaching the land surface. As he was entering the atmospheric region of Earth, the wave that was pushing him up started to get weaker.

Adro anticipated that he might again be pulled back and it would be impossible for him to get out. Just then, a wave which was about 15 times more powerful than the latter pushed out Adro from the lake.

Adro flew out of the lake, bringing out some water with him and landed on the ground. It took Adro sometime to settle down after this sturdy push from the lake.

Adro was lying down on the ground with his hand held tight to the slimy liquid. He got up from the ground, with the dirt stuck to his soggy clothes. He looked at his hand and found the slimy liquid on his hand. "At last I got this." He said to himself.

He took a 360 degree view to check if anyone had spotted him with this unique material in his hand. "I guess this had made this lake go mad." He said, looking at the lake which was now calm. "If this could do this much to a lake, what would it do to a man?" He asked to himself.

Adro now was able to keep this substance inside his pocket. So he did the same and left the place before anyone could spot him.

He knew that his house was not too far but 10 kilometres would take a lot of time to walk. "Exercise early in the morning." He said, glancing at his water proof G-Shock watch which was replaced with the watch which could have made things easier for him.

As soon as he reached home, he took out a plastic cover, which he used to collect and keep in the laundry room and took out the substance from his pocket. After being exposed to the atmosphere, the substance slowly started to lose its sliminess and became more of a liquid than a semi-liquid.

He then spilled out the remaining water from his Aquafina water bottle and carefully poured the substance inside the bottle, seeing to the fact that not even a drop is spilled out.

Adro then took a masking tape and wrapped up the bottle and kept it inside the plastic bag. He then unlocked his suitcase and hid it inside and closed the case. Due to the stickiness of the liquid, Adro rushed to the washroom to freshen up.

Adro was overwhelmed as he had discovered something different, something new, something that hadn't been imagined or found ever. And he knew that he could do something marvellous with this.

But what Adro never knew was about the potential of this liquid. Did this liquid really have something different in it or it was just Adro's assumption. Would this liquid be helpful or be detrimental to the world?

The turning point

❄ ❄ ❄

Adro had now reached Masnesia with his only suitcase and his liquid hidden inside it. As he got out of the airport, he booked a cab and then came a Toyota Innova, ready to take him to his desired destination.

"Take me to New Creek." He ordered the driver. The driver nodded his head in agreement and moved on. New Creek was the location meant for the wealthy people and Adro had brought himself an accommodation at the heart of the city.

It was a 30 minutes drive up to his home and Adro was eager to open his suitcase. He took out his house keys, which he had kept inside his pocket and unlocked the door.

As he pushed the door, he was happy to get back home. Adro rushed to the first floor and kept his suitcase in the biggest room of the house, which was a sea facing room and of course, the room in which he used to take a nap. For a single person, a 5 bedroom house would look big but with Adro in there, he is the best person who could utilize his resources to the maximum.

He had assigned one room as a guest room, so that if he had any sudden guests, they did not need to feel uncomfortable. He then had kept the second room, which was the second smallest room as his office, where he would, in his terms scribble his ideas and imagine unreal stuffs. That's where he had all his Ipads, laptops and computers set.

The third room, which is the third biggest room after the guest room was the games room, where he would play indoor games like table tennis, carom board, chess and darts. He would mostly play this with his friends and neighbours.

The smallest room was dumped with grains and toiletry stuffs. It was the storage room and Adro decided that to make this room useful too, so he had to keep something in it.

After keeping his suitcase in his room, he gently took out the plastic bag and went downstairs and kept it on the table of his office. In the same office, he had created the Peeda gun.

After keeping it on his table, Adro left the room for lunch. He had prepared a simple chapatti and Dhal. Chapatti was nothing but just an Indian bread, prepared by the mixing of water and wheat flour and Dhal was simple lentil soup.

After his lunch, he came back to his office and locked his view on the plastic bag. He was relieved that it was in the same position as he had left it.

He himself didn't know why but he felt that this liquid could change him if he had consumed it. This though came to the mind of Adro from nowhere. He felt that if this liquid present in the lake could make it so powerful, then what effect it would have on humans.

In the last week of his stay, he had inquired about the lake from some locals around that region, but no one had any complain about it. They only said that over the months, the colour of the lake started to change. From navy blue, it started to change to dark green and no other inconvenience was observed by them.

So Adro felt that the behaviour shown by the lake at that time was only because of the liquid.

Adro walked towards his closet and opened it. Inside the closet were all the mechanical and technical equipments needed for Adro. He searched through the closet for a minute and then took out the object he wanted.

Out of the closet came a syringe on Adro's left hand. "Yes." He said, holding the syringe with left palm held tightly on it.

He then walked back towards his table and placed it. He then took a seat and was ready to implement his idea to life.

"So let's do it then" He told, and removed the Aquafina bottle from the plastic bag. He then ripped of the masking tape and unscrewed the cap of the bottle. He then poured the liquid in a beaker, so that it would be easier for him to pour it in the syringe. So he did the same.

As he was pouring it in the syringe, he thought to himself, "Will this work? Or am I going to spoil myself." He started to wonder and then he answered his question, "I am ready to take the risk." And then went on to fill the syringe.

Adro was very careful on each and every step he took on his experiment. After filling up the syringe, he was now ready with the liquid in it.

He was a bit sceptical on the success of his experiment and on top of that, he didn't have any hypothesis in his mind about how this would work out. He never thought what would be the further complications he would face. He just wanted to try it out.

Adro brought the syringe towards his left arm, as he was a right handed man and injecting himself on the left hand would not make it difficult for him to do his daily work.

Adro was tensed, but he still tried to fool himself. As he was bringing the syringe closer and closer, his heartbeat started to increase rapidly.

Adro stopped for a moment and took and tried to settle himself. He then looked at the ideal spot to inject the syringe and pierced it through the flesh of his left arm.

He didn't swab his arm with an isopropyl alcohol, which is used to soften patience's skin, due to which the needle pierced through his hand caused him a lot of pain.

But surprisingly, as the liquid entered the body of Adro, the main was getting mitigated as the colour changing liquid was entering his body. Adro was taken aback as he felt that as he was thinking in his mind that the pain should go off, the unbearable pain just left the body of Adro, as if it hated staying there.

But just as all the liquid got into his body,

he started to feel dizzy and just as it got over; Adro couldn't control himself and lost hold of the syringe from his hand.

Adro quickly ran towards his room as his vision was getting blurry. "What is happening to me?" He was frightened by what the aftermath of consuming the liquid would be. He was about to collapse down. He never thought deeply about what this could probably do, but maybe it was late for Adro to repent.

Adro now couldn't stand properly nor control himself. Even the 25 meters he had to walk towards his room felt like as if he had to walk 25 kilometres.

As he reached his room, he was almost about to give up on walking further and thought it would be better to collapse down on the floor. "Just a few metres Adro" He said, he couldn't even speak as dizziness was eating up his energy.

Just as he reached his bed, he collapsed down the mattress. His eyes were shut instantly and he was now in the mood of hibernation.

6 hours went by and Adro just got up from his sleep. His vision was still blurred and he couldn't see things that clearly.

Adro got up from the bed and sat on the sofa next to his bed. He was still not able to come out of the giddiness and felt uncomfortable. He took his kettle placed on the coffee table which was in front of his sofa. He lifted the kettle and filled his glass, which was next to the kettle with water.

As he was filling it up, the water started to spill around the table. He then lifted his glass and took a sip of it. Adro wasn't able to fully gulp the water as he started to feel that the colourless substance had a very bitter taste. The water couldn't stay inside his mouth even for a second and he spit it out.

Adro sat back on his seat and tried to adjust himself. His head was spinning and he just didn't feel good.

Adro stood up and tried walking towards the drawing room. He then had a look at the newspaper and saw the picture of Entric Cooper, A famous musician who used to sing pop songs and always used to roam with spikes on his hair.

The newspaper stated that he is making a new album called Impossible. Adro stared at his image for 45 seconds. His body was still and his eyes glued on the picture. He suddenly felt like someone had pushed him from behind and he was standing still to absorb the shock.

Adro had never listened to the songs of Cooper, but by just staring at him, he came to know everything about him. His past, his songs, his present work, location and also what he is thinking now. "He is going to have a concert in this country after 2 months." Adro uttered unconsciously.

"What's happening to me? Why am I suddenly saying this?" He wondered. "I have never seen this guy before and how come I know about his songs, bands and other stuffs about his."

Adro sat on his sofa and switched on the Television. Co-incidentally, on the TV channel he was in, they were talking about Entric Cooper.

Adro was spellbound to listen that Entric had just announced a minute before about his tour to

Masnesia and that he would be having a concert there in 2 months.

Adro immediately switched off the TV and had no words to express his feelings. He looked at his hands, which became weak and filled with stains of the ink of his pen, which fell as he was writing down his ideas onto his book. After which, his hands were now messy and his body weak due to the experiment.

Adro only looked at his hands, covered up with the dirt after completing his experiment and also soggy due to having contact with the weird liquid.

He was also weak and tired and also filled with giddiness. "I need to get energized and neat." He thought and it happened just like what he wanted.

Starting from his hands, his body underwent transformation. He was able to change himself. From being weak and feeling dizzy, he soon started to feel energetic and enthusiastic back again.

Even his physical parts of his body could undergo transformation and they did so. The mark that was caused due to the injection was like as if Adro never seemed to have injected himself. He hadn't taken a shower the whole day and now he felt neat, clean and active.

Adro looked at his hands with happiness. As he was looking at it, he started to give out a wicked laugh. His expressions and voice modulation had changed and he had started to depict an attitude of a guy filled with evilness.

Adro's assumption was indeed right. He had got the superpowers in him. In fact these types of powers to shape shift would have only been seen in our imaginations. But now, Adro was inhibited with this distinctive feature.

Not only could he shape shift, but could also gather other's thoughts, memories and feelings. He could also transfer the mind of another person to him and know about their history, present and also their present thoughts and moves. In other words, he now would know what others are up to and anticipate and think in their way. He could now have everyone under control on his fingertips.

But the problem this liquid had on Adro was that it was extracting the mad side of him. The liquid was making Adro into a devil by activating his evilness. Now each and everything that Adro used to do smartly, he now would achieve it by adding his evilness. But what we all have to look forward to is, if Adro would be able to win the war with the help of his powers and his evilness?

Adro knew that because of Hobad, he had lost his lab and his fame. The normal Adro would have dealt with this in a calm and strategic manner but the new Adro wasn't for that type of a route.

"Hobad" He screamed "I am coming for you." Adro couldn't think calmly and it seemed like now, Adro's evilness and anger couldn't be removed. Adro was now with only one goal, to retaliate to Hobad's destruction. This is to now play his moves in the war, the war which would go down as the war between the two.

Curves can't be Straight

* * *

Back in Hobad's office, the CEO was having a busy time in the last 3 months. He had to shut down the making of the Banana Wardrobe as the technical errors were too complicated and was impossible for even the best heads in the company to rectify it.

Hobad had then sent out an apology letter to the whole world regarding the problems caused by the Banana Wardrobe and promised that Banana Electronics will see to the fact that there isn't any major technical fault and there never will be another one.

This statement received positive reviews from people all around the globe and Banana Electronics were able to regain their customer's trust

Luckily no one sued Banana Electronics for this and all the cases regarding this issue were cleared. Hobad was now ready and also increased the confidence of his employees to make the Banana ITab a success.

Hobad's fear was about Adro. He was first afraid if Adro would file a case on him, claiming the Banana Wardrobe was based on his idea or give Hobad a taste of his own medicine, which was to sabotage his company. But Hobad was confident that Adro would never even dare to take up that move.

But whatever treat Adro had to offer to Hobad was least expected by him, which was a Tit for Tat.

Hobad was now in his cabin, playing chess on his laptop. Just then, "Tring Tring" Hobad's phone rang. Hobad loved the sound of the old telephone and decided to keep that sound as his phone's ringtone.

Hobad picked up the phone and found it to be an unknown number, but still he went on to pick it up. "Hello" he greeted but there was no response from the caller. "Hello" Hobad said again and still there was no response. Hobad got furious, "Hello can't you hear me" he shouted.

The caller gave a loud laugh. "Hi Hobad." The caller whispered, "Getting angry isn't good my friend." He replied. "Online games can be played afterwards too."

"Now look at your company." He continued, "Your ITab won't last long." He said, with a wicked laugh. "How do you know about the ITab?" Hobad asked. "I never disclosed this to anyone." The caller replied, "No one told me, but people should have an eye on their enemies, right?"

Hobad was now getting agitated, "Who are you?" He asked. The caller just kept on giving his wicked laugh and then paused, "The name is Whyson, Adro Whyson."

"Adro, it's you!!" Hobad asked in panic, "How did...you.." Before Hobad could ask Adro anything, Adro said, "I am just 3 kilometres away from your office." He stated, "If you are smart enough, save your office from my destruction." He challenged Hobad.

Hobad hung the phone in disgust, he wasn't happy at this stage about the leakage of his new project. But he also was bewildered on how could Adro even know the address Hobad was in.

"He is just 3 kilometres away and he has threatened me that he might do something to my office. What would he do?" He wondered. Just then, something struck his mind. He recalled a known person of his, working for the Masnesia police.

He took his phone and was scrolling through the logbook. Just then he got the name and dialled. "Am I speaking to The Sniper?" Hobad asked, "Yes, it's me." He answered. "Tell me my friend, Hobad Doughnauts. What do you want?" He asked. He had a heavy voice and a high pitch. His voice was filled with toughness and confidence, just the right person to help Hobad out.

"Yes, I have a big problem." Hobad cried, he then took a minute to narrate the story. But in this modified story, he said that Adro was a criminal, trying to obliterate him and his company and was just 3 kilometres away from his office.

The officer was very well aware who Adro Whyson was, in fact knowing about Adro, he was about to deny the fact that Adro could do something stupid like this. But due to Hobad's influence, he had no other option but to follow his instructions.

In no time, The Sniper had organised his team to safe guard the company and also ordered an inspection on all the vehicles which passed through the office.

Just as the inspection was going on, a bearded man had entered the office of Banana Electronics; he went to the foyer and walked towards the reception. He claimed himself as someone known to Hobad and wanted to meet him desperately. The receptionist had called Hobad via the intercom and said, "Sir, Mr.Woodrow Cataflam wants to meet you." Mr. Cataflam was in reality Hobad's uncle who left the country 10 years ago and never ever was in touch with Hobad and his family, but Hobad was snobbish and it was his nature to keep people waiting. "Tell him to come in another 15 minutes." He ordered

Mr. Cataflam only had a backpack with him. He didn't look neat but ironically, after he had suffered great losses in his business he had chosen, he turned up in a red Mercedes SLS AMG.

He then partially opened his backpack and in there was the Peeda gun. On the Peeda gun was a small foldable screen. Mr. Cataflam unfolded the screen and then it came to life.

He then went on to type some codes on the screen and then clicked the enter button.

'Ready to fire' Read the screen, which was the digital brain of the Peeda gun. 'Please pull the trigger of the gun to continue.' It continued.

Mr. Cataflam left no time and pulled the trigger at once. He then closed his backpack as he could see the green liquid bubbling and this assured that the gun was busy in its work.

He then zipped up his bag and walked towards the receptionist and said, "you can cancel my appointment." He said. "I will meet him afterwards."

The receptionist agreed to the request and did the same. Woodrow left the place at once.

As he was about to get into the car, the sniper spotted Mr. Cataflam and felt suspicious about him. He ordered one of his men to go and inquire about that man. He felt, why would Hobad ever meet an untidy person. He was wearing a dark blue coloured T-shirt with stains of ketchup all over it.

"Why have you come here?" The police man asked Cataflam. "I had come here for some personal reasons sir." He replied.

"What type of personal reasons?" the police man inquired again. "Sir the personal reasons are too personal." He replied, dodging the question of the policeman.

"Then tell me your name." He inquired. Cataflam was silent; he then switched on his watch and clicked on the app 'My Car'. He then was busy looking at his smart watch and tried to open the boot of his car. The inspector was irritated and again asked, "Tell me your name?"

As the door of his boot started to open, Cataflam replied, "Check it out." He said and soon Woodrow Cataflam started to change physically. His bearded face was replaced by a clean shaven face. His dirty T-shirt, with stains on became into a red Polo T-shirt and his eyes were covered with Lacoste sunglasses.

Adro threw the bag inside the boot of his Mercedes SLS AMG and closed it. He quickly ran towards the driver seat and left the spot at once.

"There is Adro, there is Adro." shouted the inspector. The sniper spotted the red colour vehicle and commanded them to follow it.

Just as all the police cars allocated to chase Adro were on their task. Adro didn't hesitate to make a call to the tensed Hobad. "Hello Hobad." He said. "Looks like you have deployed an army to catch me?"

"Don't try going anywhere Adro. Because your final destination has already been finalised by me." He threatened.

Since the time he had injected himself with the weird liquid, he had developed a wicked laugh which was too haunting for anyone to hear. "See Hobad, You might try to put me behind bars, but you always fail to understand me."

Hobad started to scratch his head in confusion, "Stop scratching your head Hobad." He said. "How did you know I was scratching?" He asked. "First have a look at your company and then try to catch me." As soon as Adro finished saying, he cut the phone and then changed his gears.

From Hobad's office, it was indeed a long chase. Adro knew where he could possibly end this chase and decided drag on this interesting cat and the mouse chase.

Adro started to drive on the highway, with the speedometer showing the speed as 230 kilometres an hour. The speed lights were flashing at Adro, but he never cared. He was now a criminal, with the goal to vanquish Hobad and company.

Hobad's PA came running to his cabin and said, "Sir, this is terrible." Hobad didn't like it when he always had his PA running towards his cabin and only giving him bad news. "What is it?" He asked.

"Sir, our factories in India and South Africa have caught fire."

"Stop bluffing." Hobad shouted. "How could both the factories catch fire at the same time?" He asked.

"But sir, I am telling the truth." He said, showing him some pictures about the accident, taken by the employees over there.

Hobad was speechless. He took deep breaths to control his emotions. The factories set in India and South Africa were producing about 95% of the products of his company and the destruction of these main factories means that Banana Electronics would be incurring huge losses now. Hobad told his PA to go back to his cabin and he sat back breaking his head on who could have done it.

Just at the right time, 'Tring Trring.' His phone rang again. Hobad grabbed his phone and answered, "Adro! Stop irritating me."

"Wow, the CEO of Banana Electronics has lost his cool!" Adro replied in a calm and composed manner, as if no one was behind him. "Take it as a gift from me." He added, "Now let me enjoy the treat you've given me."

Adro threw his phone away by drawing down the left side screen of his car. He then started to trick the police by changing the lanes continuously. He then decided to increase the difficulty level to catch him.

Adro decided to now change his path and drove through the roads of Dronefera, which was the most crowed areas in Masnesia.

Adro was still ranging at the same speed and didn't bother if cars were blocking the area or not.

He would bump into another cars to make his way, damaging it or he would perform exhilarating stunts and pass through the traffic.

The police were losing Adro as he somehow made his way through all the traffic. But then came the difficult part for Adro. His view had taken off the arrogant smile in him, which he had as he escaped each police vehicle and each gunshot with ease. But this now meant that Adro was nearing the end of his chase.

He started to reduce the pace of his car as there was a traffic signal ahead of him with the lights at red. The police felt that Adro was now trapped and he had no chance to go beyond this traffic.

"Block the free exit." The Sniper commanded through the walkie talkie. The road was now filled with cars waiting in lines, for the signal to turn green.

Adro had other plans, as he started to slow down his speed to 80 kilometres per hour, he quickly tapped the button, 'Stunt Mood' on his car's monitor.

All the officers were observing Adro and waited for the moment when he would stop his car.

Suddenly below the chassis of his car arose something no one would have ever expected. Adro again went on to increase his speed back to 230.

Below the chassis came a single wheel which was connected to the frame of the car.

All the four wheels stopped working and the car began to balance itself on the lone wheel. The car moved at the same lightning speed even though it had only one wheel doing the work.

But one move Adro did to escape the traffic had stunned everyone on the road. As he was moving on, the car started to increase its height and as Adro approached the cars which were stationary, waiting endlessly for the signal to go green. The Merc was now about 5 meters above the ground level.

The lone wheel made its way through the tiny pathway formed between two cars and also drove between the cars passing through the transversal lane via which the vehicles, which had been given a go ahead by the traffic signal, could pass through.

Adro passed through the lane with ease, giving a shock to the drivers who were waiting for the green light and for the ones who were given a go ahead.

He got his car to the normal height and was still on the move. Adro had escaped the claws of the police and he was beyond the sight of the fleet.

The Sniper was speechless. He didn't know what to do next. He had lost track of Adro, even in which could be the most advantageous situation for the force.

"I have never seen anyone as equipped as him." He said, feeling disappointed about the result.

He called Hobad and informed, "Sorry Sir, We have lost him." He said. Hobad was incensed. He was clueless on how could a person like Adro escape from one of the strongest police force in the world. How was he able to guess what Hobad was thinking and was going to do next.

Right away, Hobad had come up with an idea to trap Adro. He then cleared his throat and resumed the talk "Listen to me carefully Sniper." He said and shared his plan which he felt could be the best to execute Adro.

As he finished sharing the plan, The Sniper agreed for this. "See my friend." Hobad said, "This should not be in cooperation with the police." He said. "This is my problem and I want it to be conducted without the help of the police. I do not need your help nor need your help to arrange it. I can manage this by myself." He said

"Then why are you sharing this with me?" The sniper asked. "Because I want to tell you that you aren't that capable to do such rough tasks." Hobad said, teasing the sniper. "Don't get involved in it and not allow the police to intrude into our clash." He made himself clear.

An annoyed Hobad was gnashing his teeth. He banged his hand on the table and said, "Adro, Your game is over. Your plans and over confidence will go down in vain."

The free fall

* * *

After an exhausting chase, Adro reached back home at five minutes to eight in the evening. He did feel tired but he indeed enjoyed tackling the police vehicles and the public traffic.

He took out his backpack from the boot of his car and climbed upstairs and kept it in the closet of his office, along with the Peeda gun. He then removed his watch and his gloves and placed it inside the first drawer of his desk

He then walked downstairs towards his open kitchen and picked up his silver cup, which he had purchased in Chennai. He filled it with water and went on to gulp it.

But just as he brought it towards his lips, his instincts made him to spill out the water into the sink. His body was not ready to take in the liquid and Adro was agonized on this response from his body.

"Oops I forgot." He thought to himself and kept the cup aside. Adro closed his eyes and started to feel the transformation inside him.

Adro opened his eyes and now felt energetic and his enthusiasm was pumping to its highest point. "I haven't slept nor eaten anything since the past 3 days nor do I feel like doing so." He said, staring at the vegetables placed on the basket next to his cooking stove.

"At least let me try taking a nap." Adro ran upstairs to his room and lied down on the bed at once. He covered himself with the blanket and tried to give himself some rest.

"I have been busy thinking about achieving my goal." He said. "It was not easy to set in that extra wheel in the car."

Adro didn't feel like sleeping but still did cover himself with the blanket. Just as Adro was about to doze off, he got up from his bed and walked towards his office.

Adro was in there for a long time. He had also taken his night clothes with him which were folded and kept neatly.

Adro had shut the door of the room and never turned out. Nor was there any noise heard from inside, except for the noise of the sewing machine and the crumbling of papers.

45 minutes later, Adro came out of his office room with his night clothes and his previous attire in his hand. He walked towards the laundry room and threw the clothes in the basket, even though it wasn't necessary for him to do so as his shape shifting powers could also clean his clothes up.

Adro went back to his room and was asleep. 12 hours later, at eight in the morning. Adro's eyes slowly started to open and Adro started to get a view of the roof.

But this wasn't the roof of his house; this roof

was curved Adro felt like as if he was in an elevated state. He felt that he was in a different bed. Compared to his, this bed was smaller and the bed was made out of steel, which was completely different from the bed of his, made with wood.

He then tried to get up, but he couldn't. His hands and legs were tied up to the bed using a rope, making it impossible for him to move. "Who is this?" he cried. "Why have you guys captured me and what do you want from me."

"Shushhhh Mr.Whyson." The voice of Bolten Dewar. He was a stout man who was wearing a blue shirt and an Indian accent. He was Hobad's most trusted henchman who had done all his work to perfection. Hobad felt that other than involving the police and directing them to do so, Hobad wouldn't have the pleasure of executing Adro in his own way.

He had kept his goons aside, so that the police don't interfere at that moment and give Hobad trouble. Now he had informed the sniper about his plan and also requested them not to poke their nose into this.

"So today, your game is going to get over Adro." Bolten said, sitting on the chair which was next to Adro's bed, giving Adro a better view of that person.

"Where am I?" Adro cried in fear, "Leave me, what do you want from me?" He pleaded. "Nice acting Whyson." Dewar commented, "But this time you can't escape."

They were inside a jet plane, with all the seats ripped off and the plane virtually empty, except for just two seats, which were placed close to each other and in one of those two seats was Bolten sitting.

Excluding the pilot, Bolten was the only person inside the flight with Adro. Hobad asked him to take in few more people with him but Bolten denied the suggestion and said with confidence, that he as a single person was enough to execute Adro.

"We had just taken off and you woke up immediately." He asked. Adro didn't reply to it, he was applying his full force, but couldn't.

"Now we will take you to a forest and then... You're over." He continued. Adro stopped him and just then he knew what to do.

Adro interrupted Bolten and said, "Bolten Dewar, It was nice meeting you." And with the implementation of his powers, he was able get himself more muscular power.

"How do you kn..." Before Bolten got a chance to ask him about how he got to know about his name, he was taken aback by Adro's power to get himself out of the ropes which were so tight that even a well built person couldn't get out of it with ease.

Bolten didn't know what to do immediately. Just as he got his right hand to his pocket to remove out his piston, he was knocked on the face by Adro, who took no time to get up from the bed and knock the man out.

Unexpectedly, Adro was too strong for Bolten. He was not able to handle the knocks on his face. As Bolten caught his hand on his piston to have a shot on Adro, he kicked of the gun from his hand and punched him on his stomach.

With every punch, Bolten was jeopardising into a worse state, with his body now getting weaker and weaker.

But then, unexpected by Adro, he started to feel dizzy and was about to faint at the flight. His head started spinning and he was not able to think properly.

Bolten felt that it would be the perfect moment to give it back to Adro. He got up from the floor and steadied himself to give it back to Adro. He ran towards Adro and pounced at him.

Instantly, Adro regained his consciousness and energy back and then, moved away from his position. As Bolten couldn't control himself, he fell down on the floor.

As he escaped Bolten's punch, he found himself standing near the piston. As soon as Adro found the piston lying down, he picked it up and pointed to piston towards Bolten.

Bolten was now frightened as he was about to get shot by his own piston, which he considered lucky. "One" Adro started the countdown. "Two, and..." Adro didn't say three, he was aware that just behind him was the door and he only had to pull the lever which was just next to the door to unlock it.

Adro diverted Bolten's attention, frightening Bolten with the piston and slowly, he tried to pull the lever without having a look at it.

Just at the right time, he was able to pull down the lever and unlocked the door of the flight. Adro opened the door and suddenly, there was a sudden change in the air pressure. Adro and Bolten could barely withstand the strong suction being felt.

Adro took this as the right opportunity and shot at Bolten's chest, 'Bang' and Bolten collapsed right away down the floor.

"Sorry Bolten, I was just too smart for this." Adro commented and jumped out of the plane. Just as he jumped out, he aimed at the engine of the flight and then shot thrice, 'Bang Bang Bang.'

As Adro was freefalling from the flight which was 15,000 feet about the ground, the engine instantly caught fire and it spread all around the flight in no time.

The plane was left burning while Adro jumped out of it without any parachute with him. But just as the doctor ordered, popped out the pilot chute from the back of Adro's night clothes.

As he was approaching the ground, the parachute came out from Adro's shirt, making his landing safe.

Last night, Adro went to his office as he knew about Hobad's plan and also knew that Bolten would come into his house and take him on the flight.

To create an escape plan, Adro was drawing rough diagrams about his ideal parachute, but it didn't come properly on paper. After some tries, he got it right and had inserted the parachute inside his night clothes.

Adro had now reached the ground safely, thanks to his super powers. But he did start to wonder why he suddenly felt weak and exhausted.

"Should I consult a doctor?" He asked himself. Adro analyzed the situation and felt that if he goes to any hospital or public area, then he might get caught.

"Okay then, let me now figure out how to go back home." He said, "I manage the rest afterwards." and vanished from the place at once.

End-Less

* * *

Three weeks went off in a spark and Adro was getting weaker and weaker. He was not able to swiftly think or use his powers. He used to always buffer while making even the simplest decisions.

Adro didn't feel good. In fact, after taking in that horrendous substance, he had been having a difficult time with his body.

He felt that maybe these symptoms faced by him would be there for a short duration and then it would disappear. But unfortunately it did not happen like that.

Adro's powers were also getting diminished day by day. He was not able to rejuvenate himself or gather Hobad's thoughts. He was feeling helpless and restless.

One fine day, Adro abruptly decided to go back to Chennai and have a look at the lake from which he had obtained these powers.

Adro got himself his forged documents ready to escape from the police. He tried his very best to shape shift into an imaginary person, but he didn't have the superpowers to do so.

With the little he could, he had changed his

colour of his eyeballs from black to light blue. He had also grown himself a thick moustache. He had travelled by the name of Jack Gollaso.

Adro travelled again in economy class, this time he was getting himself adjusted to it. In his trip, he didn't bother to know what Hobad was up to and just wanted a peaceful environment.

As Adro wasn't able to energize himself by his powers, he decided to have a sleep in the flight. After days, he was able to sleep peacefully, not to fool or execute someone. He wasn't worried about anyone tracing him nor was he bothered if they did so. He wanted to be the normal Adro but sadly this power fluid has now turned up to be venom which was killing him.

Thus Adro had made up his mind not to use his powers, this decision brought Adro to the worst state. As he avoided knowing and anticipating Hobad's next moves, Hobad had kept his traps ready for him.

As Adro exited the Chennai International airport, he was greeted by Hobad's goons waiting for him. He had a friend of his known as the commander, who had kept his goons well placed to catch Adro.

Hobad was aware due to one of his informers, that Adro had left for Chennai and also changed his looks too.

So immediately Hobad had called up the commander to catch Adro and narrated a plan that sparked out of his mind. The commander agreed to the given plan and carried it out.

In Chennai, Adro had taken a Suzuki Baleno on rent. Adro took out the car from the parking and drove off. He wanted to have a look at the Hash Brown Lake, the lake from which he had obtained his powers and felt that he needed to have a look at it before he succumbs due to the liquid.

Adro pressed the accelerator, making the car speed through the highways of Chennai. But what was now troubling Adro were the two Mahindra Scorpios which were following him from the time he left the Airport.

Out of the blue, the two SUV's became four. Two were behind him and two in front of him. Adro was not given a chance to change his lanes either. Now he had a total of eight cars around him. Two forward, two behind him and two SUV's at either sides. All the cars were of the same model and of the same colour. Except for the number plate, no other differences were to be seen in the car.

Adro tried many ways to dodge them. He tried changing his speeds abruptly to somehow trick the drivers and make his way out. But he failed in doing so.

He knew that he was followed but sadly, he wasn't able to get his whole mind to make a way to tackle the situation. They were professional drivers who were assigned to trap Adro.

Adro gave up in getting out of this given trap and decided to follow them and instead go to the place taken by them.

Adro was so mentally unstable that he couldn't figure out Hobad's plans.

Two hours went, and Adro was still followed by those goons. All of a sudden, all the SUVs which were surrounding Adro all of a sudden vanished.

Adro was first relieved about the disappearance of those vehicles but as he went on, he realised that he was now in an unknown region. There was nothing except for lush green plants all around and just a tar road in front of him that went on endlessly and a railway track, which was about a 100 meters away from the road Adro was on.

That Railway track was the path at which the Shatabdi express from Chennai would go towards Banglore.

Adro had now reduced his speed as the place looked alien for him. All of a sudden, a Ford Endeavour came in between the road from the lush green land and banged over the Suzuki Baleno. Not able to withstand the force, the sedan toppled over and Adro found it difficult to come out of the car.

Adro tried his best to come out of the car and he did so. Adro's vision was now blurred and his hands and legs injured badly. Blood was flowing out of his body and the pain was awful.

"Who are you?" He cried, not able to withstand the pain. Just then came out a man, wearing a leather jacket on his white T-shirt and blue coloured wrangler jeans.

He removed his sunglasses and threw it away. "Hobad! You?" He screamed. "Yes Whyson. I have come to bid adieu to you." Saying so, Hobad came close to Adro and jabbed him on his face. Adro couldn't bear the trauma he was going through.

Adro had all the resources, but his mind was

switching off. Adro had his watch with him, but never thought about using it. It never struck his mind that he was wearing it. He had left his Peeda gun back home in Masnesia city. Adro had nothing with him.

Adro's body didn't cooperate with Adro. As Hobad was giving him his punches, which he yearned to do for a very long time, Adro started to feel uneasy and started puking. His vomit was very gruesome and disgusting.

The vomit had a blend of fluorescent green and white waste. As he was vomiting further, the vomit too started to change its colour. Sometimes it would stay green, then purple, orange, red, yellow and so on.

Adro was dehydrated; he was so feeble that he would faint any moment. Hobad took advantage of it kept on hitting him on his hands, legs and face.

Adro was now kneeling down; his eyes were shutting down while his view of Hobad was getting blurry. "Now let's finish the nuisance off with this punch." Hobad boasted, looking at his fist.

Hobad locked his aim at Adro's face and swung his right fist, which he considered as his strongest. Surprisingly, Hobad had missed his target as Adro ducked it.

Adro now couldn't do anything else. A frustrated Hobad walked towards the boot of his car had took out a sow.

"You have no moves to play Whyson." He said, knocking Adro once again with a sow. Adro collapsed on the ground, not able to bear the pain further.

Hobad knew that Adro would not be able to

get up for a long time and didn't bother to check his pulses. Hobad dug out the lush green soil.

He then dug out the soil, enough to bury Adro in. After placing him inside, he covered up his body with the soil which he removed, leaving no evidence behind.

Hobad had also reported this incident to the police stating that he come to Chennai for recreation and then he had found this damaged car, which met with an accident and when he checked in, the driver was not to be seen.

The police believed Hobad's statement and Hobad was able to tackle this particular issue. He had now won the game of chess abolishing Adro Whyson and his name.

People considered Adro Whyson a criminal, who was a psychopath trying to abolish Hobad Doughnauts and Banana Electronics.

People never believed it in the starting but when Hobad narrated his cooked up story to get the whole world to go against Adro and be in favour of Hobad.

After executing Adro, Hobad has had the best time of his life. Banana Electronics got the Banana ITab into the market and it had got Banana at the number one position.

Two years have gone by and Hobad has been able to crush each and every enemy of his in just a matter of seconds but Adro was the only toughest and oldest competitor he had and had also finished him off. His only concern was Eprun, thinking that he might cause a big chaos again. So he found a perfect executer and demanded the Commander to finish Eprun too.

But what no one, even Adro was never aware of was that his body still had about twenty percent of the liquid flowing in his body. Out of the liquid Adro consumed, only thirty five percent of the liquid gave him the powers while the other sixty five percent was present to give him a tough time.

The liquid inside Adro's body kept him still alive and also prevented his body from decomposing; this liquid truly had the magical part of it working and at last, it had helped Adro in a positive way.

Adro didn't have any energy in him and decided to lie down on the ground with his upper part covered with soil even though he was not going to get rotten. With Adro termed dead by the world while in reality he was alive, what was going to happen next? Would this war continue or was it Hobad, who won the prolific game.

He is always there

* * *

There was still two hour left for Eprun and Junward to reach the Bangalore central. Making use of their time, both the individuals dozed off.

Eprun was fatigued after attending a busy meeting back in Chennai and also after narrating the whole story about Adro Whyson to Junward.

The train was travelling peacefully, while suddenly the outside weather began to change. The grey clouds started to cover the region where they were travelling.

Incidentally, they were 35 kilometres away from the point where Adro was buried. As the grey clouds covered the sky, it started to pour.

It started to drizzle and water dropping on the lush green plants. Just at the moment, there was a loud noise of choppers being heard.

From sitting inside the compartment, it felt like something was falling down on the train. The sound came once, then twice, then thrice. Like that the sound came five times.

All the passengers were sickened to hear the type of annoying sound and this happened only in one compartment and in that compartment was

Eprun and Junward.

While everyone were puzzled from where this sound was coming from, just then two people entered from the back entrance of the compartment while another two entered from the front entrance of the compartment.

The four of them with their revolvers in their hand, they all were approaching towards one point, they walked towards Eprun and Junward.

Just at that time, when the droplets of water was splashing on the ground, the top soil started to shake vigorously and then a hand shot up from below.

The hand tried to clear of the dirt which was obstructing it to be free. After clearing it up, the hand then gave way for the face to come out and then it did.

Adro Whyson's face was covered with mud and his clothes were partially rotten. Adro got up slowly and tried to stand on his feet. But it was really difficult for him.

Adro glanced at his left hand and saw his watch working smoothly. He was perplexed when he saw the date and year shown by his watch.

"What?? I am in 2016?" He asked. He knew that his watch couldn't show the wrong time and date as this feature is connected to the satellite and the time would change depending on the place.

"2 years have just gone in taking rest." A disappointed Adro said, with his voice stuck with dirt inside, making it very difficult for him to speak.

He then could feel his long beard, which had grown up to his chest over the years and his long hair. He looked like a man in the Stone Age.

Adro then looked at his state and told to himself in his mind, "I shouldn't have injected myself with that stupid liquid." He started to repent.

At that point in time, an idea struck in his mind, "Eureka, that's it." He thought to himself, "How could I forget this." and closed his eyes in concentration.

He tried hard and stood still for a long time, just as he was trying his best to use his powers. It had completely slipped out of his head that he had this powers in him and felt that it would have been great if he would have utilized it against Hobad.

In the train, Eprun and Junward were now trapped with the four goons surrounding him. The fifth one came in late from the front entrance of Eprun and Junward. Here came the Commander.

"Stop playing the Whyson's tricks." The Commander grinned at Eprun. He then clapped his hands and ordered, "Lock him." The commander said, pointing his fingers at Eprun.

Eprun and Junward were both equally horrified to see revolvers surrounding them. "Let's begin the countdown." The commander ordered.

"Somebody help us." Eprun cried in fear. He was helpless as he had nowhere to run and the revolvers were just a centimetre away from the both of them. Even if they made a small move, they would be shot on the head.

"Someone help." Eprun shouted again. Unluckily, Eprun couldn't move his hands so there was no chance in pulling the red chain of the train nor did anyone dare to help them out.

Back in the grassland, Adro was giving his hundred percent to energize himself but every time the transformation took place, it would happen up to his elbows and then stop.

All of a sudden, Adro was able to hear someone screaming for help. Adro spotted out that the sound came from a train and also noted the compartment.

Adro's mind was now functioning like the same way it used to, but he was now physically weak. The Commander was now in the middle of the countdown, "Four" he shouted, "Three, two ..." Just before the Commander could count one, inside the compartment entered a man who came in flying.

The passengers had their eyes glued at Adro. Due to his long beard and hair, which had some moist sand stuck on his hair?

"Who are you now?" The commander asked. Adro didn't reply. He closed his eyes and gave his full concentration. Soon, his muddy skin started to glow; his damp cloths were becoming neat and tidy. His body started to regain energy and his long beard disappeared and his hair got back to his normal length.

"Adro ?" Eprun cried. The Commander too was surprised as he was the one who was involved in getting Adro trapped to Hobad.

"I don't reply to unintelligent questions." Adro replied, attracting two out of five revolvers with his gloves in perfect condition.

The Commander ordered his men to attack the strong and energized Adro, who had become the same intelligent and smart Adro Whyson which he was and wanted to be badly after the mystical liquid got into his body, spoiling him.

But Adro now had fresh moves for newcomers. Knowing that other than the commander, only two others had their revolvers with them.

Before the two of them could pull the triggers, Adro shot two bullets at each of them on their ribs.

The two of them collapsed at once. The Commander was the only person left. Adro, who near the entrance of the train, which was opened as always, threw both the revolvers outside the train.

He then speedily knocked off the revolver from the Commander, keeping the both of them equal with weapons in their hands.

The frustrated Commander was very well ready for the combat. He first tried to give a punch, but Adro ducked it, making the commander even mad.

The commander tried to knock Adro once again, but Adro, making full use of his regained strength also made the Commander miss that opportunity too.

Adro felt that he was dragging things too long and decided to wrap up things. "Mate, you have wasted your opportunities." Adro said and then punched down the commander on his face.

The Commander fell down instantly, not getting up again. Adro lifted the well built man with his full might and then walked towards the nearest entrance of the compartment and threw his body out.

In this part of the train, people come over to feel the breeze while now; a person's body was thrown out in the breeze.

"Phew! That was heavy." Adro exclaimed, walking towards the seat of Eprun.

"Hello Eprun." Adro greeted. "It's long time since we've met." He said casually. Eprun was overwhelmed to see Adro back. When the whole world stated Adro Whyson to have been dead, he was stuck in the outskirts of an Indian state.

"Adro where were you?" Eprun inquired. He was speechless after seeing Adro. "I was here for the past two years with new friends." Adro replied in his sarcastic manner.

"What?" Eprun asked.

"Leave it, you won't understand." Adro replied with a laugh.

Eprun had introduced Junward to Adro. Junward too was dumbfounded at what he had witnessed for the last fifteen minutes.

To spoil up the good mood, Adro started to feel uneasy again. "I need air." He gasped for air. "I need to use the restroom." He pleaded and then ran towards the restroom and closed the door. He started to vomit continuously for five minutes. He vomited out a substance which had a blend of green and orange.

After puking out the substance, Adro felt relaxed. He felt like a normal man, the type of a person he wanted to be badly for a very long time.

After coming out of the washroom, a passenger, who was in the same compartment and also in the first row from the washroom asked Adro, "Take some water."

The man handed over his bottle of water to Adro. Adro was thirsty and exhausted after the fight, he had gulped half of the bottle.

"Thank you very much." He replied and gave the bottle back. As the water started to travel into his body, Adro's face was now filled with smile.

After two years, he was able to eat or drink something and it was also welcomed by the body.

"I am normal." Adro reassured himself. "I am normal once again." He said in happiness, knowing that the evil and the supernatural powers of Adro had now been taken off, much to the happiness of Adro.

Check mate

* * *

After reuniting himself with Eprun and the World, Adro Whyson had gone back to Masnesia to settle himself.

Adro was back to normal. As he entered back home, he was relieved to get back home as the old Adro. The man who had lost his real self had got it back in the same country.

He walked around his home, reminiscing the time when he had never fallen prey to that gruesome inhuman substance. Adro did learn one lesson from this, which was not to be greedy of power and position to be different from others. The loneliness felt by a man to portray him as different would bring a person down by a great deal.

Now he had to pay back the difficulties faced by Adro. He was able to escape from the jaws of death but now it was the right moment to check mate him.

Adro never bought himself a new phone so that he could avoid pointless calls. Five days later, Adro had got himself out of his house, exposing himself to some sunlight at four in the afternoon.

Adro was searching for his favourite Mercedes SLS AMG, but then recalled that he had left the car back at the airport two years back and by now, it would have been towed away.

Both of Adro's cars were either destroyed or left behind indirectly due to Hobad. But Adro loved the German automobiles. His Audi was vanquished, His Merc was taken away. Now was his third and final car, the Beamer.

Adro grabbed the car key of his 2013 model BMW 5 series and left his garage and got himself back driving on the roads of Masnesia City.

It was just a matter of moment and Adro was back to the same driver he was. With the sun setting down, his suave driving skills displayed on the road were a treat to watch.

At sharp six 'o' clock, he had reached the building, 'The Prez towers'. Adro did have a very good memory and also was able to remember the information he had obtained from other's memories. As Adro had used his powers to obtain the memory and thoughts of Hobad the most, he also got to know his residential address.

Adro got into the lift and clicked the button which took in the command and accelerated to the 72nd floor. As he got on to the 72nd floor, he entered the penthouse of his sworn-in enemy, Hobad Doughnauts.

Hobad meant nothing for Adro but since he had to go through mental, physical and social torture, Adro knew that he had to give it back.

Hobad's door was opened and Adro got into it with no problem. As soon as he got in, a bodyguard came in front of Adro and did a security check.

"Is Mr. Doughnauts there?" Adro asked the bodyguard. After finishing the check, the bodyguard replied, "He is at the balcony."

"Thank you" Adro replied and marched towards the balcony. As he was walking, he was stopped by the bodyguard. "Why do you want to meet him?" He asked. "Who are you?"

Adro turned back and replied, "I am a well known person of his." He said. "He will recognise me in an instant and it won't be necessary to tell him my name." He said, taking out his spectacles from his coat and wearing it and followed his path towards the balcony.

As informed by his bodyguard via a walkie-talkie, Hobad was expecting the unknown guest to meet him at the balcony.

Hobad was standing in his balcony, staring at the skyscrapers of Masnesia, which reminded him about his success in life and how he was relating himself to the tall sky scrapers.

The balcony was as huge as a palace, stretching from one end of the penthouse to another.

As Hobad was lost in thought, "May I come in Sir?" came a voice from the back of Hobad. He felt that he had heard this voice somewhere but was not exactly able to figure out who it was.

Hobad turned back and was taken back with astonishment. He couldn't believe that the person he had executed a couple of years back had come back to life.

"Is that Adro Whyson?" He asked. "You

guessed it right Hobad," He replied. "May I come in?" He asked again and Hobad told him to come in and have a seat.

Hobad too took his seat and they both were sitting opposite to each other with a coffee table between them.

"How did you comeback Adro?" Hobad asked.

"By flight." Replied Adro.

"So you're trying to give smart answers to me."

"No, in fact I am giving."

"Stop acting smart Adro" He ordered

"I don't need to do so Hobad. Because that's what I am."

Hobad raised his eyebrows in astonishment, "So took a long break didn't you?" He asked. "You reached Chennai with a thick moustache, now your back to Masnesia with spectacles." Hobad laughed.

"Adro, don't attempt to apply the same tactics done by your opponent. He will surely succeed." Hobad continued to laugh.

Adro didn't react anything for what Hobad said, he too joined Hobad in the laugh. By looking at Adro give out a wicked laugh daunted Hobad, taking off the smile in him.

"I guess you seem to enjoy yourself a lot." Adro commented about Hobad's lifestyle. Hobad didn't get what Adro was trying to say but then observed through the glass panel that his bodyguards were out of sight.

This sudden disappearance of his bodyguards started to make Hobad tensed. "Why are you tensed Hobad?" Adro asked. "You have the Tagoplasm in you, you shouldn't worry about anything."

Hobad started to panic, "How did you come to know about Tagoplasm?" He asked. Adro ignored his question and continued further, "Why?? Does that still remind you of your best friend, Doctor Tag?"

Hobad didn't know what to do? He now started to sweat in fear. Tagoplasm was the most confidential information about Hobad and as far as what Hobad was aware of, Dr. Tag couldn't have told this to anyone and had no personal contact with Adro.

Hobad knew only one solution was left with him. The solution was to execute Adro instantly.

Hobad took out his gun from his back pocket, pointing it on Adro. "I should have killed you at that moment itself, but now it's all over." Hobad said and went on to pull his triggers.

Just as he was above to do so, Adro had clicked a minute red switch which was set on the handle of his glasses.

Hobad's gun flew off from his hand got into the hands of Adro Whyson. "Hobad Doughnauts." He called out, "These moves by me would have surely made you go nuts." He said and pulled the trigger.

The bullet hit the left shoulder of Hobad and then came out the red colloid that Hobad never expected it to come out.

Adro fired another one at his chest, pierced through the body of Hobad, which had never been victim to a single injury.

Adro got up from his seat and said, "Mr. Hobad Doughnauts, it was pleasure playing this game with you. Check mate." He stated.

"If you want to really figure out how Tago-plasm was deactivated." Adro continued, "Then that's mission impossible." He grinned. "For now, feel the pain."

As Hobad was dying, Adro removed his spectacles and threw it on the floor, causing it to break. "I don't need this anymore." He said, walking out of the balcony and leaving Hobad fighting a losing match.

Adro's enemy went out to execute Adro, but sadly got himself trapped into the jaws of death. Adro now had no enemy, no identity.

He was considered dead by the whole world and no one would believe him if he went out to claim himself as Adro Whyson. Even if he succeeds in doing so, he would be put behind bars.

What Adro would do next, all rested in his hands. But now, Adro was a free man. He had no one to trouble him nor did he have a track record, which would be troubling him.

Adro was now himself; He was the King of his self created universe with no one to oppose him. It was only him and his decisions that were given the most importance.

He was now in search of a peaceful place, where he could start his new journey with a new identity.

The talk

❄ ❄ ❄

Somewhere in the World,

The courier man arrived at the given address at eight in the morning. He rang the bell of the majestic three storey mansion, which placed on top of a rustic mountain, facing the huge blue sea.

The courier man was captivated to look at the marvellous structure, where he had come to deliver the package.

As the door of the house opened, the man inside the house had spotted the courier man and asked, "Yes, can I be of any help?"

"Are you Mr. Waltic Walsh?" The courier man asked. The man nodded his head and said, "Yes, I am Waltic Walsh."

"Then here is the book you ordered." The courier man handed over the package to the man, took his signature and went away.

The man was planning to go out and was getting himself ready. He was wearing an ordinary shirt and shorts, which were made of the material nylon.

He took the package, opened it and then took

out the book he had ordered. Keeping the book in his right hand, he walked towards his newly purchased Porsche Cayenne and got inside the car.

He kept the book on the front passenger seat, which was to his right. He accelerated the pedal and the car started to move.

As the man was in the middle of his drive, he hurriedly searched for a phone number. As he was scrolling through the phone book, he found the number he was looking for. He then dialled the number via the car's Bluetooth system.

Adeep was trying to solve some mathematical problems in order to prepare for his upcoming unit test.

Just then, he could feel his table vibrate. He knew that someone was calling him and with his phone in silent mood and the door of his room closed, he felt this to be the right opportunity to pick up the call.

"Hello" He attended the call, "Who is it?"

"Am I speaking to Adeep?" the man asked. "Yes, it's Adeep on line." He replied.

"Oh that's great then." The man replied. "I had purchased your new book, The war between the two." He said.

Adeep was filled with happiness, "Wow, did you read the book?" He asked in excitement. "Yes I did." The man replied.

"Any comments?" Adeep asked the man once again. "Where?" The man asked back, dodging the kid's question. "I beg your pardon." Adeep asked back, not able to understand what the man told. "Oh this boy is too soft in his head." The man murmured to himself, Adeep couldn't hear a bit of what he ever said.

"The book was great." He replied. "I personally liked the character of Adro Whyson. He does love to change his identity and fool people though." He commented.

"Looks like you do see a lot of you in Adro?" Adeep inquired. "Yes I do." The man replied.

"The story was really interesting." He continued. "It's a really good attempt from a fourteen year old kid." He added.

"Your previous book, 'I do not understand a thing' too was a nice book."

The praises from the man made Adeep happy. "Okay then Adeep, it was nice talking to you." He ended. Before he could end the line, he was stopped by Adeep by another question, "Sir I just want to know one thing." He asked, "Could you please tell me your name?"

This question brought a huge smile on the man's face. After rejoicing the question asked to him for a couple of seconds he then replied,

"It's Whyson, Adro Whyson!!"